DOWN
and
DIRTY

DOWN and DIRTY

Gammy L. Singer

Dafina
Books

KENSINGTON PUBLISHING CORP.
http://www.kensingtonbooks.com

This book is a work of fiction. Names, characters, businesses, organizations, events and incidents are either the product of the author's imagination or used fictitiously. Any resemblance to actual persons, living or dead, is purely coincidental.

DAFINA BOOKS are published by

Kensington Publishing Corp.
850 Third Avenue
New York, NY 10022

All Kensington titles, imprints and distributed lines are available at special quantity discounts for bulk purchases for sales promotion, premiums, fundraising, educational or institutional use.

Special book excerpts or customized printings can also be created to fit specific needs. For details, write or phone the office of the Kensington Special Sales Manager: Kensington Publishing Corp., 850 Third Avenue, New York, NY 10022. Attn. Special Sales Department. Phone: 1-800-221-2647.

Dafina Books and the Dafina logo Reg. U.S. Pat. & TM Off.

ISBN 0-7582-0895-2

First Kensington Trade Paperback Printing: March 2006
10 9 8 7 6 5 4 3 2 1

Printed in the United States of America

ACKNOWLEDGMENTS

I continue to be thankful for the many people that help me, support me, and shepherd me through life. I'd like to thank the girls—not referring to my breasts—but to my girlfriends who keep banging the drum loudly for me and are my biggest supporters and fans—Margaret Avery, Michelle Davison, Wendy Fairbanks, Ernestine Jackson, Emily Yancy, and smoochums, my daughter, Laetitia Russ.

I'm grateful for Unity Church of New York, which inspires me to climb mountains and the Harlem Writers Guild, which helps me navigate the mountains I've created.

Special thanks to Robert Knightly and Al Jenkins for their legal expertise and my own landlord, David Howson, for his opinions, reflections, insight and knowledge of Harlem. (If I've made any mistakes it's my fault, not theirs.)

Bless you, Rachel Rudman for the Russian phrases.

Kudos to the team at Kensington, editor Karen Thomas, Nicole Bruce, and special thanks to Jessica McLean, who has been so very helpful to an upstart newbie author. Additional thanks to my agent Frank Weimann.

Finally, thanks to the readers who have wanted to spend some time with Amos Brown—I am grateful.

Chapter 1

Three-way action. Chipmunk folded, and with a six-deuce off suit in the hole, so did I. Seven card stud poker. Five thousand in chips stacked in front of me. Since I had started with only five hundred, I figured I was doing pretty good, playing a tight game, not going crazy. A sense of propriety caused me to linger at the poker table. Not good form for me to leave so soon after amassing all these chips. I looked at my watch and yawned. I'd stay another hour.

The limits had been lifted, unusual for this group of players who regularly exchanged the same couple hundred bucks week after week, but some high rollers that Chipmunk, the host, invited swooped into the game and changed the parameters of the betting. But the rollers had long since departed, dropping a shitload of green, wagging their tails behind them and then leaving the regulars with the fever, the stakes remaining high.

I crossed my arms and watched Buster on my left push two stacks of chips to the center of the table, raising the pot five hundred more, and I caught a whiff of his polyester funk. My silk shirt, wilted now and as ripe as its owner, fared little better after thirty-some hours of poker.

I had promised myself that I would cut back on my gambling and hadn't intended to show up for the game—after all, I had a business that needed tending to. I'd been a landlord for four years now, with attendant responsibilities. Well, so much for promises. It was holiday time and I needed to be distracted.

Yep, *Christmas is the loneliest time of the year*, not the loveliest, like the song says.

I looked around me. In a storeroom in back of Chipmunk's bodega, five of Harlem's solid citizens sat around a poker table a week before Christmas. Everyone in the small room had a cigarette lit but me. Smoke crawled to the ceiling. I rubbed my burning eyes and scratched my day-old beard and looked around for a drink to appear. No such luck.

Ronnie, five foot and stacked, wearing a mini-skirt that barely covered her ass, sat on the sidelines on the top of some stacked boxes of tomato paste and ignored my unasked request. Buster, the owner of two funeral parlors and the senior member of the group, noticed and cracked, "Shit, Amos, don't expect Ronnie to get up off her butt and serve you. Hell, me and you just interlopers, smack in the middle of domestic mess." He looked across the table. "Ain't that right, Zoots? What's with you, man, you ain't said sorry to the lady? You ain't begged for mercy yet, boy?"

Zoots Cooper scowled and didn't respond. Eyes darted around the table and a few of the men sniggered. Ronnie semi-hooked for a living, but tonight she was working the poker game, taking Dot's place. Everybody at the table knew that Zoots was sweet on her. Zoots was an upstanding young man with a future in front of him, but if he wasn't careful, his gambling habit might be the end of him. As a functioning addict myself, I knew what I was talking about. That's why I gave myself rules—kept me from going over the edge.

Zoots, not yet out of his twenties, was already the proprietor of a dry cleaning and tailoring establishment, named Zoots' Suits. He put his business in jeopardy each time he played poker, an action that understandably might make a woman mad, especially somebody like Ronnie to whom money meant a lot. Truth to tell, I suspected she was just as sweet on him, but she was making him scratch for it, especially tonight, with him a thousand in the hole.

I looked in Ronnie's direction. Eye candy, she made the players feel good, more expansive, more apt to open their wallets and let the money pour out. Chipmunk knew it and that's why he begged Ronnie to hostess the game tonight instead of Dot. Dot had been around the block a few times and not quite as choice a morsel. Case in point, Dawson the Dog stared at Ronnie all night long, making mistakes and throwing his chips away.

But Buster, an instigator if there ever was one, knew that Zoots and Ronnie were an item and wanted to start some stuff. Add a woman on the fringes of a serious poker game, one who had a personal interest in a player, and you were asking for trouble.

Nine or ten players floated in and out of this weekly game. Usually the money rotated among the group members and nobody lost too badly. Except, as might be expected, the unfortunate few who regularly lost and the fortunate who regularly won. Count me in the winner category, but understand I didn't depend on this group for my bread and butter.

I still had feet in two worlds and played enough poker with the criminal element to turn a profit. But hey, I argued, they were old-style, not the gangster type, with a little more élan, a little more class than the young punks operating on the streets today, and a few of them, solid buddies of mine. But I had no compunction about Robin Hood-ing them in poker and they knew it. Take from the rich and spread the shit around was my motto.

His gold tooth winking out of his mouth Buster continued to tease, "Did you beg for mercy, Zoots?"

Zoots colored and said, "Mind your business, Buster. I call, nigger, and raise another five." He nodded to Chipmunk. "Just deal me a Jack, Chipmunk."

Chipmunk shrugged, "Sorry, Zoots, don't take requests."

"Oops, the man called and *raised me*. The youngster called me. Uh-huh. Said yoo-hoo. Said yoo-hoo and called my ass. And raised. What you got? Ain't fooling me, talking about jacks. You got to have a pair of honeys. Am I right? Too bad, 'cause I'm holding aces."

"I'm working a straight, nigger. Pay to find out."

"Oh, believe me, I'm gonna' pay to see what you got, youngster. Soon as the betting comes back to me. Hey, wake up, Dawson Dog, what you doing, man?"

Dawson had five liquor stores all over Harlem and was called Dog because he resembled a hound, no lie. Dawson raised his head out of his chest, swung his jowls from side to side and mourned, "Damn, everything going on at this table except poker. Can I get a drink? Huh? Can a thirsty man get a drink? Please?" He held up a five dollar bill and waved it in Ronnie's direction, "I'll say please, even if Zoots don't want to say please. Takes a man to say please. And I'm a man." A wink to Ronnie. "I can say it. Listen good to me, Ronnie. Baby, *please*—just like James Brown."

Dawson Dog burst into a chorus of *please, please, please*, him with a wife of thirty-five years whom he cheated on regularly with every young skirt that came across his path, singing so badly that even Ronnie had to bust a smile and she finally got up out of her seat and ambled to the bar, fleshy butt cheeks rippling like mighty ocean waves. Five pairs of eyes, including mine, oogled her ass and the red imprint that the tomato paste box had made across the back of her thighs.

"Scotch and—,"

"I know, I know, Dawson—," Ronnie said. "Ain't nothing new. Don't have to keep telling me."

Buster licked his lips suggestively and said, "Hell, girl, it's been so long since you moved that mighty fine butt of yours, how we supposed to know you remembered something as insignificant as our drinks?"

Buster's flirtation inflamed Zoots and he jumped up, fists ready, and promptly banged his head against the overhead lamp. The light careened away and its metal shade swung around in a drunken arc and cast wicked images on the table and the cards. Dawson reached up and stilled the shade while I put my hand on Zoots' shoulder and eased him back down. "Buster's trying to get your mind off of poker. Don't pay him no mind. Ronnie, bring me a Courvoisier, will you?—and give this young fool something to cool himself off."

Buster laughed again. "Aw, Zoots, I ain't mean no harm." And then he fixed his mouth to say, "Hey, you know how to get a woman to act right? Huh? You want to know how?" He paused to take in each of us sitting around the table before he roared, "Take that pork chop out her mouth." Thumping my arm, he let loose a hurricane of laughter. "Huh, Amos, am I right? Woman think she gonna' lose that pork chop, she'll do anything you say."

I shook my head. Crazy fool. After Buster settled and wiped the tears from the corner of his eyes, he rapped the table once and asked Dawson, "Okay, man, what you doing? You calling?"

Holding cards close to his nose, Dawson rumbled to no one in particular, "Yeah, that'll sure enough make her straighten up and fly right. Uh-huh." Then he leaned back and said, "Hell yeah, Buster, I'm calling. You ain't bluffing me."

"Well, put in, nigger."

Dawson laid his cards in front of him, placed a chip on top, stroked his scraggly beard for a few moments and methodically counted out his chips. Then he shuffled the chips in his hand, in military cadence, and regarded Buster. He let a minute pass before he finally shoved the stack of chips to the center of the table. Sweat beaded his forehead.

I knew he was beat right then. Buster thought so too. See, poker ain't about betting on cards, it's about betting on people. Buster sniggered, "If you got to think that long about it, man, you don't need to be betting."

Chipmunk bumped the table and said, "All right. Pot's right. Looking good. Last card, coming out, down and dirty." He dealt the final card face down to each of the players.

Suddenly, the phone hanging on the wall jangled, startling everyone. We froze.

Something about its ring, swear to God, made me know somebody was calling me. Its shrill insistence, like a scorned woman, made me think, uh-oh, trouble. I looked at my watch. Eight a.m. Play stopped but no one answered the phone, and it continued to ring. Finally, Ronnie threw up her hands and with a sigh deep as the ocean crossed over to the wall phone and snatched the receiver off its hook.

"Hello," she barked. Then she listened intently and her lips pulled down into a frown. A few seconds later she held out the receiver. "Someone calling from jail. Someone locked up in the Tombs."

All eyes turned in the direction of the phone.

"For you, Amos," Ronnie said.

I knew it.

Relief settled on the faces of the other card players and nervous laughter swirled around the room. Zoots tipped his chair back against the wall and said, "The Tombs. Man, they call that place the Harlem Hotel, 'cause half the male population in Harlem has checked in and out of there at one time or another. Amos, a brother needs you. Better answer."

Buster smirked, "They calling for the Harlem Don, that's what they figure Amos to be. Ain't that right, Amos? Ain't you the Harlem Don? Who y'all think it is? Anybody wanna' make a bet?"

"Damn, man, you'd bet on the moon," Chipmunk said.

"Glad nobody's ringing me up," Buster said. "They know better."

I dawdled, adjusting my suit jacket hung over the back of my chair before I started toward the phone.

"Hey, Amos—just 'cause somebody calling, don't mean you got to answer. I wouldn't answer it if I was you. Can't be nothing but trouble."

I glanced at Buster—on some level he made sense and I did know better. But I couldn't ignore the call—I wasn't made that way. I lumbered my six-two frame over to where Ronnie stood and with a sigh lustier than hers took the receiver from her hand.

Bad news, sure enough. I listened in frozen horror as my caller, old friend and mentor Deacon Steadwell, dripped the news like poison in my ear that he was in jail and charged with murder. In the background, play continued and loud shouts accompanied Zoots' win, a two thousand dollar pot.

Mind reeling in disbelief, I struggled to catch my breath, while only a few feet away Ronnie threw back her head in hyena laughter, oblivious to everything but Zoots and his win. Ronnie, a study in rapture, and the poker players, surreal figures in a disappearing universe, drifted far away.

Steadwell, my mentor, in jail for murder.

Chapter 2

Just because I'm an ex-con don't mean I'm a stupid mother-fucker—oxymoron or not—but it was difficult to follow what Steadwell, sitting behind the plexiglas in the Tomb's visitors' room, was trying to tell me. Eyes wild, the old coot sat and babbled into the phone on his side of the partition. But the conversation veered off into endless loops, and I couldn't get the connection between the fur coats he recently hijacked from Katz Furs—a Park Avenue furrier—and the murder charge of which he was accused.

An attempt to calm him didn't work, he became more agitated. His voice shook. The deep gouges and scratches in the plexiglas made it difficult to get a good gander at him, yet I knew the man sitting across from me in faded prison garb hanging loosely off of thin shoulders was ready to blow. Arthritic fingers clutched the phone and tears streamed down the caverns of his whiskered face.

Hard to look at misery full-blown like that. I dipped my head in the direction of the floor and waited for Steadwell's storm to pass. Dirt inched its way along the cracked linoleum, skidded past my feet and flipped over, wriggling its legs in the air. A damn bug. Damn this place and damn Steadwell's hide. Why hadn't the old man called sooner?

I scratched my forearms, nails digging deep. Visceral memories cut into my psyche, a strumming harp playing across my brain.

Being in this place gave me hives. Some things are hard to forget—being incarcerated was one of them. I shuddered, brow damp with sweat.

When Steadwell quieted I looked up—only a few snuffles issued from him now. I blamed the events of the last three months for this sorry state of affairs. Something in the air. A hell of a time. Disaster in October, Ali TKO'd by Holmes in eleven. In November, Reagan'd won by a landslide. And here it was near the end of December—and some crazy had killed John Lennon. *Who the fuck would kill a Beatle?* And now the topper, Steadwell's arrest, the culmination in a series of bad luck events. The world gone to hell in a handbasket.

Superstitious? Me? Naw . . . Well, maybe.

I followed the speck of dirt with my eyes as it traversed the linoleum and crawled in drunken zigzags up the wall. Then I turned to Steadwell and asked him straight out, "Why do the cops think it was you killed Dap Jones?"

Steadwell wiped his nose and said, "Dap had my knife."

"What?"

"Had my knife—stuck in his belly."

A whoosh of air blew out of me. I scratched my shoulder. "Damn. Dap? Dap the pimp?" I stared. "How'd they know the knife was yours?"

Steadwell's shoulders slumped so far forward they met in the middle of his chest. His head hung low, his eyes hidden. What was the cat doing? Watching dirt on his side of the partition? Shit-faced, he looked up and responded, "'Cause it be my name burnt into the knife handle."

I sucked air and scratched my forearms. The rickety folding chair which held my burly frame rocked back and forth.

"Shit Steadwell, did you—?" I stopped myself.

"No—hell, no." Anger seared past the pain on Deacon Steadwell's face. "Amos, look here, I knowed you before you had grass on your ass. I knowed you back when you was a pissant numbers banker—before you straightened up and went into the landlord business. How come you ain't know me?"

He nailed me. I said, "Making sure, Deacon. Don't take but a breath to kill somebody, and you know I know that."

His eyes locked with mine in sober recognition. "Amos—you wadn't nothing but a pup when you did what you did. A mistake. But old as I am, look here, what'd be the point?"

Then he answered himself, " . . . besides the fact the slimy mother-fucker needed to be killed."

I glanced over to the guard posted outside the door, who hadn't moved a muscle. "Talk like that don't help your cause."

"I ain't done it, Amos, that's the God's honest truth—you know me." Steadwell wiggled like a worm on a hook. "But that don't mean I ain't wanted him dead. The fucker stole my fur coats. *Stole them*. All nineteen of 'em. Minks, sables, ermine. That no-good skeezer took 'em."

Ironic, a thief getting robbed. Steadwell boosted—had, for as far back as I could remember. The man stole anything—from a pickle to a Plymouth—but he'd always been lucky. He'd never seen the inside of a prison—until now. Never been arrested. And what galled him most was not the jail time he faced, but the fact that a goof like Dap outsmarted him.

Used to be, nobody put nothing over on Steadwell. I remember when we met—me, stupid and thirteen, trying to hustle hustlers, two heavy-duty hoods who worked for Sweet-lips Dorsey, the reigning policy man in Harlem. Steadwell slid into the action, smooth as silk, and saved my black ass from being decimated.

See, Steadwell knew every con trick in the book, and worked them all. To be flimflammed by Dap Jones hurt his pride. He caught me smiling and snarled, "This ain't funny worth a damn, Amos Brown."

"I ain't laughing. Dap getting over on you—put it down as the price of doing business, ain't that what you used to tell me?"

Steadwell's eggplant complexion changed to apoplectic purple and he screamed, "Ain't you never heard of honor among thieves?"

"Heard about it, ain't never seen it—apparently Dap hasn't, either."

Steadwell's next words caught in his throat. He choked and sputtered. His sputters escalated and turned to hacking coughs. And then he gasped, chair flying backwards, and next thing I knew, he had fallen to the floor in a heap. The thump of his chair stirred the guard to action and he hurried into the room, weapon drawn, undecided whether to shoot or help the fallen man.

I tapped against the Plexiglas to get the guard's attention. "He's fainted," I shouted.

Eying me suspiciously, the guard holstered his gun and uprighted the chair. Then he shook Steadwell. Down the row of cubicles the curious angled their heads and bodies to get a peek at what was going on. Steadwell moaned and thrashed on the floor but didn't revive, so the guard went to the water cooler and returned with a Dixie cup of water and dumped it in his face. Steadwell sputtered and the guard pulled him up to a sitting position but putting Humpty Dumpty together was difficult and Steadwell kept falling over.

When Steadwell's eyes finally rolled open, the guard eased the old man back into his chair, all the while glaring at me as if it were my fault.

The guard, a decent sort, asked Steadwell if he needed medical attention. Steadwell became indignant, and shook off the guard's help. I told the guard that Steadwell didn't need him anymore and would probably be all right. The guard hesitated for a second and then moved away. No skin off his nose.

Steadwell's arthritic fingers clenched the Dixie Cup. The man had deteriorated—no doubt about it—since I had last seen him—August, I think it was. Steadwell had to be eighty or close to it, but his skin had never looked this slack nor his body this broken down. He suddenly looked his age, and it was disturbing to see. Prison time? No way he could survive. Steadwell didn't belong here. I had to get him out. I tapped against the glass. "Pick up your phone, Deacon."

Bewildered, he looked at me as if I were a stranger and then he slowly picked up the dangling receiver and pressed it into his chest.

"Are you all right?" I said. He nodded. "Listen, man, do the cops know about the coats?"

"Cops say the coats are motive—say that's why I killed him. I said, no, it weren't motive, but that's how come Dap came by my knife. Bastard stole it when he stole my coats. See, Dap heard about the coats and came to my house, puffed up like a fat cat, and told me he had contacts and could fence the furs for top dollar. He wanted to talk about it some more and offered to buy me a drink down the street at Smitty's. I went with him and had a drink. And then I had some more. He left me sitting at the bar, and when I got back to my apartment six drinks later, my damn coats, money, watches, and other assorted inventory were gone."

I thought to myself that didn't mean it was Dap stole his coats, but I kept quiet. No use upsetting him further. But in Steadwell's eyes two plus two equaled forty—and Dap was the culprit.

"Okay, look—button up until I can get you an attorney. Don't talk to no one."

"Don't need a lawyer. Got a lawyer. What I need is to get out of jail."

"Whatever lawyer you got hasn't done you much good, that's why your ass is still in jail."

"What am I going to do, Amos?"

"Jesus, Steadwell, how come you waited until now to call me?"

Steadwell's face twisted and he said, "'Cause I kept thinking the police would see their mistake. But then the Grand jury indicted me. My arraignment's tomorrow. What am I going to do, Amos?"

As if I knew. "I'll get you a new lawyer as soon as I can," I said.

Steadwell's eyes blinked rapidly and his hands shook again. I couldn't have him fall apart on me. I parroted to him what he used to say to me, "Take it easy, greasy . . ."

"Yeah, yeah, I know—and let things slide. In case you ain't known it, Amos, things be sliding all right, sliding straight into the crapper, and taking me with it. Fuck the lawyers—you can get me out. You the Don of Harlem, ain't you? Tell them cops they made a mistake, Amos."

His faith was touching, but he had thrown a Superman's cape over my shoulders and expected miracles. I told him, "Doesn't work that way, you know that—but I promise I'll help."

Steadwell's face broke into a million pieces and he beat the table in front of him and screamed, "But I been framed."

"Steadwell, be cool."

Just then the guard advanced on us and hauled Steadwell out of his seat. "Easy," I told the guard. But the old man kicked and wailed and as Steadwell was being led away, the other visitors cast baleful looks at me, as if it were my fault again that the old man was bawling. From the open hallway Steadwell shouted, "I ain't done it, Amos. You know I ain't kilt nobody."

What's black is sometimes blue. What's fact is sometimes smack. Fact was, I didn't know, not really, no matter how much Steadwell protested.

I left scratching, knowing I couldn't let the old man rot in jail— not me.

Chapter 3

Over the bridge and through the woods . . . I crossed out of the Tombs, across the Bridge of Sighs, into the Criminal Courts Building, and took the elevator down. In the early afternoon outside 100 Centre Street snow tumbled out of the sky in a repeat performance of last night and its lucent brilliance contrasted sharply with the gloomy bleakness out of which I had just come. I turned up my collar against the chill. Manhattan was blanketed in white. Sharp winds howled like ravenous wolves through the downtown corridor.

Steadwell's call caught me unprepared. Two days ago, it was tropical New York—okay, that's an exaggeration, but the trench I had on was a joke. I was not properly dressed for this turn of weather. Thank God my wool pinstriped suit offered warmth, even if, at the moment, it was rumpled and reeked of stale tobacco.

The wind furled my coat and it flapped behind me like sails on a ship. I struggled to button it and mourned that my burly warm coat hung in my closet at home at 247 West 128th Street. Home. I sighed and looked down. Useless to click my slick Stacy Adams shoes together because no matter how I longed for it, I couldn't transport myself magically home, and these kicks were a joke in this weather, not made for tramping through snow.

Sugar, my newest ride, barely two months old, black on black with leather seats, glossy wood dashboard, and a prodigious stereo system, had been left in front of the Hotel Cecil up in Harlem under a mound of snow. The car was just too sweet. That's why I named her Sugar. I hoped her hubcaps remained intact and wondered whether anyone would be lame enough to dig her out of the snow and steal her. These days? You never could tell.

I shot a look at my watch. Better get to getting. Frost blew from my mouth as I walked hurriedly down the steps of the Criminal Courts Building. Had to catch that lawyer. Could have called on a pay phone inside the building, but hives propelled me and I couldn't wait to vacate that whole scene.

I turned north to Chinatown. My shoes ripped farts in the snow with each scrunch of my size twelves. Weight heavy as rain clouds rode my shoulders as I trudged. Before long, my feet were soaked and my hands burned from the cold—and me with no gloves.

Shit. I stopped on Canal Street at the nearest telephone booth, hopping back and forth on both feet and with frozen digits dialed a familiar number, that of Prince Allan Higgans, Esquire. My breath sucked razors, and my body agitated like a washing machine. How the fuck had it gotten so cold so fast?

I stamped my feet, cupped my free hand and blew into it. An answering machine came on and I left a terse message. Me, I didn't chat with machines, not in zero weather. Okay, okay—I admit I owned one myself, a handy tool in the landlord business, but the impersonality of it all bugged me. If I was ten light years behind the rest of civilization, so what? Anyway, I came from the streets, where business was done face-to-face. See, I like to see people's faces when they lie to me—especially about their rent. Fill in the blank. "Mr. Brown, I can't pay you because . . ." I hung up the phone and sanded my hands together.

The sky was slate-gray and clouds hung low and crowded me. The wind bit and snow whirled about me. I followed the example of the other pedestrians and averted my face as I hurried to the nearest subway station. I wasn't crazy—stupid, neither; let me get to home-sweet-home before the storm got any worse.

The wind shoved me from behind and deposited me into a subway entrance. I descended the stairs and at the bottom I shook myself like a dog shakes water and touched the tip of my nose. In that short spate of time, an icicle had formed and drooped off its tip.

People surged past me in a rush, and I rode a wave of humanity across the subway platform and into a number 6 train heading uptown.

Communal breathing frosted the train windows, and the heat from the car as well as from the crush of bodies made me want to holler momma. This Dante's inferno was worse than the cold. Suffocating, I ripped open my coat and jacket. The woman next to me frowned when I elbowed her. Air. I needed air.

The train paid no attention to my discomfort and lurched and ground along the tracks. A new best friend pushed up against me, and nestled his newspaper against my chest. The print was upside down, but still, I managed to read the paper's headline, a game most New Yorkers play. "No Suspects in Diamond Jewel Heist." Huh, and what about a fur heist? Did Steadwell make the news? I angled my head to read more.

Best friend snuggled closer, his paper digging into my neck. Butts, shoulders, flanks—the many cuts of beef—pressed against me as the train lumbered steadily uptown to Harlem.

I tried to ward off the discomfort by closing my eyes and thinking of something else, and the ride gave me time. To think, if not to breathe, and the clattering sounds of the tracks coincided with the clattering in my brain. Who killed Dap Jones? If Steadwell didn't do it, who else would want him dead?

Dap sometimes boosted—that was no secret—but his main deal was pimping. But economics in Harlem these days were tough. Nowadays the prostitutes competed with the addicts. Druggies would go down on somebody for a quarter, and give up booty for a dollar. Everybody and they momma was tricking, seemed like, price slashing a bitch. No surprise if Dap looked to build revenue elsewhere. Sure, why not hit up some unsuspecting booster like poor old Steadwell?

But Steadwell couldn't be sure it was Dap that did the deed. And who had the coats now? The police?

Steadwell was correct—no honor among thieves, not anymore. Harlem was in the middle of a fucking epidemic. City Hall, the police, and the politicians had turned deaf ears and blind eyes on the drug problem in the city.

Harlem was a war zone, and good people were leaving. Me, I couldn't leave. My bitch, this Harlem, good or bad. Knew its every block and corner. Wasn't I born right there at Harlem Hospital—on the corner of 135th and Lenox? Housing Urban Development was supposed to take this community, raise it up, and what did they do? Built a damn garage. All that fuss over the State Senate Building, and the city ends up building a damn garage. And what about the people's needs?

Meanwhile, I fought daily to maintain what I had while looking to the future, and a lot of my energy was devoted to keeping the drug dealers off my block and out of my buildings. Crack houses, like goody-palaces, had surfaced all over Harlem. I'd closed the deal on my third piece of property, another brownstone located just one block over—and the ink hadn't dried before I found out that two crack houses, independent of each other, had set up shop on the same block and were doing a thriving business.

Another one, a block east of those two, did business directly across from a drug rehab house, of all places. Well, shit, you could see the sense of it—bring the product to the client. Long lines, resembling welfare lines, snaked around the block each and every day. Sunken-eyed zombies roamed the streets, their twitching bodies ready to score come hell or high water. The streets were a battleground, and the enemy lurked within.

Every time I hit the streets nowadays I carried a piece—a palm-sized .25. Didn't have it on me now—told Zoots at the poker game to hold on to it for me. Which reminded me. Better get it back from Zoots—tracking through the streets carrying a wad of cash could be treacherous.

I fingered the neat roll banded inside my jacket pocket, five thousand in poker winnings. I always kept my money neat. Respect money and it will respect you is what I always said, and I had a healthy respect for it. Each denomination lay close to its mates, no stuffing of bills here and there. I folded it, banded it, and kept it separated from the contents of my wallet.

Time to strategize a route from subway stop to home. A shame to think that way, didn't have to do that growing up. Even in the middle of the Depression, people weren't as desperate. White people lived in Harlem when I was growing up. Drugs. It was drugs.

Property values had taken a nosebleed dive, and banks had even redlined the area. Most people couldn't get loans if they wanted to, and white property-owners let their buildings rot. No skin off their backs. Tax-wise, everything was jake for them.

I purchased my newest acquisition with cash money, thanks to a horse named Slowpoke. No dummy, I converted my winnings into something real—like *real* estate—and *real* quick, before I fucked up and gambled it away.

See, I don't kid myself. I'm clever enough to stay more ahead than behind on my winnings, but I know I'm still a gambling fool. Nothing for me to bet on something stupid, like whether the sun would come up tomorrow.

Huh, maybe in some secret way, maybe that's why I despised the druggies so much—there but for the grace of God . . . I hated them for their weakness and myself for mine.

The train screeched and came to a stop—a hiss, and the doors parted. I unpried myself from the other passengers, got off, and surfaced to the street level and looked about. Snow was piled high and, what with the brewing storm and no buses or cabs in sight, I put on my don't-fuck-with-me scowl as I leaned into the gusts pounding up the 125th Street corridor.

Shoes sodden, I passed shuttered shops gone out of business, and walked up Seventh Avenue—past twitching and swaying zombies tucked under doorway overhangs. I turned on my street, and was taken aback to discover yet another boarded-up house on my block, its owners, the Swanson family, gone. Man. That hit me in the gut. When had they disappeared?

I stood in front of the vacated brownstone for several minutes, mourning, I think. It was like staring at a fresh grave in a cemetery. *And they were so young, too*, I thought. When I reached home I was depressed.

The rent from 127th Street could wait. I wasn't in the mood. Besides, it was snowing, I was freezing, and it'd be madness to go up against some of the crazies on that block without my gun. To be wasted on a hummer by some crackhead, another Harlem statistic? I didn't think so. Uh-uh, the rent could wait.

The stairs leading up to my brownstone were icy—I held fast to the railing. Hmm . . . did I have enough coarse salt in the basement to throw on the steps and the sidewalk in front? More snow expected tonight. No point in shoveling. Well, maybe I'd better take care of the steps—they were dangerous.

Then I turned the key to the front door, stepped into the foyer on the parlor floor, and ran into Wilbur, a tenant and one of the gayest caballeros you'd ever want to meet, mincing down the hall-way stairs.

Wilbur squealed when he saw me and shook me by the arm as if he were clanging a bell, before I even got into the building good. His usual Texas drawl had New York panic in it as he said, "Mr. B., Patty's come back and threatened to take Josephine."

Since Wilbur was first-cousins with Drama—and was, you know, one of them homos—life for him wasn't nothing but a stage, with him the star. Things that flipped Wilbur out on a regular basis had to be weighed carefully to determine what was the real deal and what wasn't. Don't get me wrong—Wilbur wasn't bad people. I had gotten used to him—almost. But the thing is, well, you never knew what to expect with Wilbur.

At the moment, his horse of a face looked frightened, his eyes wild. I told him to calm down, and ushered him into my office, located at the front of the building.

When it rains . . .

I sighed and flicked a look up to heaven before entering my office, because, no doubt about it—Wilbur's news on top of Steadwell's meant December was solidly shot to shits. Deck the halls, Mo'Fo'.

Wilbur flung the muff he was carrying—that's right, a damn muff—on my couch. A dark and furry thing that resembled a gray rat or squirrel or some other rodent motherfucker. I stared at the muff, then back at Wilbur. What could I say? I bit my lip and drew blood. Yes, I was used to Wilbur, but that didn't mean he didn't irk the shit out of me.

I told him to take a load off, and also made myself comfortable, easing into the swivel chair in front of my desk. Wilbur dropped like a bag of wet cement, crossed his legs and perched on the edge of the couch, hands knitted together on his lap. Fido at attention.

"Start where it makes sense, Wilbur," I said.

"She came back, Mr. B."

I sighed heavily. "Well, Wilbur—it's not like we figured she wouldn't be back."

"Four years. Mr. B., nobody's seen hide nor hair of that girl since she took off four years ago. I thought she was dead, didn't you?"

"Where she say she'd been?"

"L.A., getting herself together."

"Did she succeed?"

"What do you mean?"

"In getting her life together."

Wilbur sniffed like he smelled shit and smoothed his processed locks. "The girl looked like bad news at breakfast."

I didn't ask him to explain, his meaning evident. I waited, and Wilbur continued. "Said she was going to Children's Services. Said she'd get a court order if I didn't give her daughter back."

Then Wilbur went loop-de-loop. Some men pound their chest. Wilbur? Wilbur beat his knees. "She can't do that, Mr. B., Josephine belongs to me. I been taking good care of her—you know I have." Each smack to his knee drove another point home.

I held up a hand. "Slow your roll, Wilbur—we both know Josephine isn't legally yours. Have you ever thought that maybe it's for the best? She's six now—when she gets older . . . there'll be problems. I mean, how's she going to explain you?"

That gave him pause. Wilbur's mouth formed a small but significant "O."

"I thought you were on my side, Mr. B.," he said.

"I'm on Josephine's side, and you should be, too. Wilbur, face it—if Patty's got herself together, she's got a right to her own kid."

Horrified, Wilbur looked at me like I had just mortally wounded him. I stirred uneasily.

"All right, don't look so betrayed," I said, sneaking a glance at the phone. Wilbur was obviously freaked, but I needed to call that lawyer.

"Look, I'll find Patty and talk to her. Might have been easier if you'd just gone ahead and adopted Josephine."

Wilbur made an impolite sound and sneered. "C'mon, Mr. B., nobody's going to let a gay man adopt a child."

"If Patty's strung out, why not—?"

"Why indeed," huffed Wilbur. "They'd put her in foster care first."

A look passed between us.

"Besides . . ." Wilbur said and stopped.

I prompted him. "Besides what?"

But Wilbur set his mouth into a thin line and clammed up.

No sweat off my nose, I thought. The silence grew between us and became uncomfortable. Finally, I said, "Look, Patty couldn't possibly want her child to end up in foster care. And if she does go to the authorities, how's she going to explain you taking care of Josephine for so long? My bet is, she'll do nothing. Where's Josie now?"

Wilbur sighed. "Hospital."

"Sick again?"

Wilbur nodded and his processed hair flipped forward; with a toss of his head, he flung it back. That's when I noticed.

"Oh, for God's sake, Wilbur—what's that gunk on your eyes and face?"

The fool pretended like he didn't hear me and said, "Sickle cell doesn't go away, you know. Josie scraped her knee yesterday—a little cut, and she's in the hospital." He stood up to leave.

I blew out a sigh because I knew Josie's disease was hard on

Wilbur, but I wasn't going to let him get away with dodging my question. "Your face. What's up with it?"

"What? This? Eyeliner, some mascara, that's all . . ."

"Have you lost what little mind you have? Aw Jeez, Wilbur, that stuff makes you look like Little Richard. Don't you get enough flak as it is about being a—?" I caught myself.

"Being a homosexual, is that what you wanted to say, Mr. B.?"

"Hell, no, I was going to say, being a faggot, fool. Why you want to make things more difficult for yourself?"

Wilbur tightened his jaw and laid a hand against one hip and said, "Mr. B., puh-lease—"

Wilbur didn't get it. I held my head to stifle the pressure that was building. "Wilbur, Wilbur, Wilbur . . . you're not just a tenant—you're a friend. A friend I wouldn't want to see get hurt. Why give these numbnuts out on the street a reason to kick your ass?"

Wilbur's face burned and he marched to the door, "Better get myself over to the hospital—"

The door slammed behind him and then there was only silence. I stared at the door. Wilbur was standing behind it. Then, after a moment, his footfalls trooped back up the stairs.

Sometimes I made sense, even to Wilbur. Good. Take that gook off his face. I leaned back in my chair and stared up at the familiar stain on the ceiling, and swiveled back and forth. God—Steadwell, Patty, Josephine—what next?

Then I bolted upright. I'd better call that lawyer now.

Chapter 4

The third ring, Prince himself answered. "Where you been, man?" I said. "How come you didn't return my call?"

A silence, then, "I called you back. Your answering machine didn't pick up."

I glanced down at my machine. He was right. Damn, forgot to turn it on.

I slid past an apology and ran down Steadwell's problem. And then it was his turn. I heard shuffling of papers. Then I heard muffled voices. Then I was put on hold. What the hell. I waited a few minutes, looked at the phone, and wondered, had I lost the connection?

When Prince finally returned to the phone, he said, "Sorry, don't have time for another case now, Amos." A few tocks of the clocks ticked by while I let Prince wait this time. Outside, a garbage can rattled loudly. I wheeled my chair over to one of the twenty-foot windows facing the street and peered through the slats in the blinds. Nothing. My garbage cans, lined against the low iron gate that separated the thems from the us-es, stood, all in a row, undisturbed.

When Prince didn't hear a response from me, he pussy-purred in my ear, "Amos? You understand, don't you?"

"What I understand, Prince . . ." I said, "is that you have a short memory." And then I hung up.

In flashtime I called another lawyer. Prince wasn't the only fish in the pond. No answer. Holidays—nobody in their offices. I made two more calls and didn't have any better luck. Didn't the lawyers know that criminals and Christmas were made for each other? Somebody ought to be in an office waiting on a call. *My* call.

My watch said four o'clock. Shit. A sudden bump in the hall outside my door made me freeze, and I stood stock-still and breathed in the quiet that followed.

And then my phone rang loud and shrill. I flipped my answering machine on and pressed my body against the door, listening. No sound from the hallway. Uh-huh, somebody up to no good. I waited, still as death, shackles rising on the back of my neck. After a few seconds the stairs creaked and my body tensed. My voice on the answering machine broke through the stillness, and bleated loudly.

"A one and a two, you know what to do."

I looked at the machine. Okay, guilty. I left stupid announcements like other people did. No matter—I crept over to the filing cabinet, reached in a drawer and pulled out a .38mm revolver. I loaded it with a box of rounds found the same drawer, then stole back to the door.

A bump—this time coming from further up. I swung open the door. Somebody tiptoeing high above on the third-floor landing. Well, I knew my tenants' footsteps like the back of my hand—or the back of their feet. Wilbur was the only tenant on top. Zeke, the voodoo man on three—death took his ass out, feet first. That wasn't Wilbur creeping, that was for sure.

I mounted the steps carefully, gun held low by my side, the stairs sighing under my weight. As I rounded the second landing a voice squeaked, "Stop. Don't come any closer—I'll blow your fucking head off."

I hesitated only briefly, and gambler that I was, bounded up the stairs and arrived on the top landing just in time to grab the intruder's belt buckle as he reached skyward for the swing-down ladder that would scuttle him up to the roof.

I jerked him back and he crashed with a thud. When I kicked him in the ribs, he yowled bloody murder. Then I dropped on top of his chest, throttling his scrawny neck with one hand and grinding the .38mm into his skull with the other.

He begged, "No, no, please don't shoot—don't shoot."

"That's right, whine. Give me more reason to shoot your ass," I said and bore the gun deeper into his bony head. Beads of perspiration exploded out of his pimply face. I was ready to pop him.

An image from long ago swam in front of my eyes. Another boy. Sweat dripped from my face and landed on his chest. My heart rat-tatted like a pneumatic drill and heat steamed from my pores. I wavered—wavered between the heaven to come and the hell I knew. Finally, I rocked back on my heels, panting, and lowered the gun. Fuck it, this barnyard piece of shit wasn't worth it.

The asshole blubbered, "Mister, see, I-I was looking for DL— but I ain't fount him." His hand folded under his back.

"You ain't 'fount' him, turdball, 'cause he don't live here and you know it. Looking to rob somebody, ain't you? Maybe some old lady, huh? That'd be somebody you could handle. Right, punk?"

I pulled him to his feet and crashed my fist into his face. A putrid smell exploded out of him, and a knife dropped from his hand. His eyes skittered to the knife. White dots of light shot in front of my eyes. Seeing his knife enraged me all over again.

I grabbed him by the collar and started shaking.

"No, no, man—please, please, I ain't mean nothing, let me go—" he said.

Wilbur materialized next to my elbow and tugged my sleeve. "Mr. B., don't. That's Miz McClendon's boy. He just a kid."

"A fucking kid with a fucking knife." I mashed the kid's rat face between the fingers of one hand and squeezed until his pimples popped. Eyes bulging, he screamed as I pulled his face close to mine and looked into his eyes. Shit. No wonder.

"He's higher than a kite. Crackhead motherfucker. Trudy McClendon's boy, huh? Where you staying? You staying at home, boy?"

"No—no—my ma ain't want me there."

No surprise. By now the stench from his unwashed body and the explosion in his pants smelled like cow dung. I grabbed him by the shirt and dragged his ass bumping and hollering down three flights of stairs. At the bottom I told him, "You bring your ass here again, won't be no next time. Stay away from my property—I mean it."

I riffled some bills from my pocket and stuffed them in the pocket of his jacket. "Get some food, you damn crackhead—for your mother's sake." His head dropped and he didn't say anything, so I yelled in his ear, "Hear me?"

He nodded, his head bouncing like a kewpie doll on a dashboard. I tore the front door open, and sent him reeling through it. His hands caught the railing, the rest of him bumped down the steps. "Next time, motherfucker, you're dead."

I slammed the door and wiped my hands on my pants. I leaned against the wall and waited for the anger to drain, my blood pressure to subside and my heart to stop pounding. When I looked back up the stairs, Wilbur was standing there, looking grim.

"You know that boy ain't going to buy no food," he said.

"Yeah, I know."

"See, Mr. B.?" he said. "See how crazy them drug addicts is? Ain't nothing they won't do for money. That's what I'm talking about. You want Josephine to be with her addict momma? Patty will get Josephine back over my dead body."

We both knew what he was talking about. We'd heard the horror stories of women who sold their own kids or prostituted them when their Jones came down. This time I didn't argue.

"Going to the hospital, Wilbur? Hold up, I'll walk with you," I said.

I stepped into the office to get my coat and gear up again, and the blinking light on the answering machine reminded me I had a message. I flicked it on and Prince's voice filled the room. As I strapped on a gun holster and stuffed the .38 in it, Prince announced that he had changed his mind and to give him a call.

So the pussy had come to his senses. I snatched up the phone and dialed his number while Wilbur fidgeted in the doorway watching me.

Charlize, Prince's secretary, answered this time, and she put me through to him in a hurry.

"Amos? Uh, sorry, man. After what you've done for me? Of course I'll take Steadwell's case."

A change of heart? I slid my tongue across my teeth. Prince was slicker than goose grease. He excelled as a lawyer, but that didn't mean I trusted him, and leopards don't change their spots. His fancy suits and Upper West Side address now lent legitimacy to his enterprises, but I remembered him when, and he knew it.

But I figured Steadwell needed somebody as slick as Prince, because every brother knew that in this city justice meant it was *just us* niggers the Man was locking up—and if Steadwell was going to beat this murder rap, Prince was the man for it.

Prince's voice interrupted again. "Amos? Are you there? I'll be happy to take the case, but of course I'll need a retainer. A thousand to start—"

"Five hundred. I'm bringing it over now."

I hung up on his objections and went to the safe hidden in the floor of the closet, pushed aside a toolbox, and popped a square of flooring up. Wilbur I trusted, so it didn't matter if he saw what I was doing. I twirled the combo of the safe. Wilbur fidgeted and said, "I need to get going."

"Hold your horses," I said. I took my poker winnings, banded five hundred, banded another five, stuffed both packets in my pocket, and stashed the rest back in the safe. I replaced the flooring, then the toolbox, locked the closet door, and remembered to hang the keys back on a rack on the wall. I smiled. Improvement can happen at any age. Misplaced keys were my downfall—I wasn't perfect.

Wilbur was past impatient, and he patted his foot and watched me as I climbed into galoshes and a heavy coat, adjusted the shoulder holster, shrugged on a wool cap and gloves. I was wiggling my fingers into the gloves when he finally blurted, "Look, I'll go by myself. I don't need anybody armed and dangerous walking with me."

"Count yourself lucky that you've got protection."

But it was on my mind as we left the brownstone, together, as bundled up as I was, if something went down, could I whip out my piece fast enough? Hell, what if I had to pee? Could I whip out Willie fast enough?

Those thoughts I erased from the blackboard of my mind and decided some things you don't need to think about.

And then I had an overpowering urge to pee.

Chapter 5

By the time I got to 72nd Street it stopped snowing but it was rough going. The sidewalks hadn't been cleared yet, but stores were open, festive in their splendor. I had stayed at Harlem Hospital with Wilbur just long enough to say a quick hello to Josie. Wilbur seemed out of it and strangely quiet. Josie's illness and Patty's return had taken a toll on Wilbur, seemed like. Stress. Let that be a warning. I should ease up myself.

Lights and tinsel decorations tricked out the West Side like a large and showy Christmas package. Not even snow stood in the way of commerce and the almighty dollar, and crowds of people braved the storm. Nothing kept New Yorkers home, not a week before Christmas.

Uptown, of course, folks existed in an entirely different universe. Harlem was bleak as a freak during the yuletide season. Ho-ho-ho in Harlem meant three whores on a corner. An occasional wreath hung from a door and wisps of lights twinkled off porches and stoops. Easy to understand why. Hard for folks to muster up Christmas spirit in a community where the residents were devoid of hope, let alone Christmas spirit, and that had begun to happen in Harlem.

Oh, the churches rocked as usual in the community, and families sequestered behind locked and bolted doors tried to embrace the holiday season, but it took an effort.

But then again, because of my no-frills childhood, perhaps I was looking at Harlem through jaded eyes. Still I couldn't remember a Christmas that brought me joy. Sad. But looking around me now made me believe God's angels made this snow, fat gobs of white whipped cream, and I had to smile. Maybe there *was* something bigger than myself.

Twilight deepened. Beneath my heavy coat, I sweated. Half a block more and I'd be there.

Brightly lit shop windows enticed as I continued walking toward West End Avenue. A scarlet slash of color caught my eye and I stopped and gazed at a mannequin wearing a stylish dress, posed in a window, one hand stretched out to me, entreating. I imagined Catherine, my used-to-be, in it. Catherine would fill that out in all the right places; the fabric cuddling the cheeks of her behind as she walked, the deeply cut bodice teasing the eye.

What the hell? How crazy was that? Eight months since our breakup, and sometimes, like now, she'd pop unbidden into my mind. And I would realize the breakup had been a sorry mistake on my part. What did Chuck Willis used to sing? *It's too late, she's gone.*

December is a hard month to get through when you're alone. No matter how much I swatted away memories, they boomeranged back. The day Catherine announced she was too good for me was a standout. Of course, she said that right after I told her I wasn't ready to get married. Irked her pretty bad. She brought up stuff about my dead mother and my dead, no-good father, raw issues for me, told me I had intimacy issues—it ticked me off pretty bad. I said some things.

To top it off, I suggested she find someone else. I remembered the hurt, angry look on her face. What the hell, I knew she was too good for me and took the path of least resistance. Today I had regrets.

The painted blue eyes of the mannequin bored into me, pity painted on her face. Defiant, I stared the mannequin down and shook off old feelings. Here I was, eight months after a breakup, thinking about buying my old girlfriend a Christmas present. Color me stupid. Who's the dummy here? I turned on my heel, and the shop and I parted company.

At West End Avenue the traffic light blinked red, yellow, green, stop, wait, go, but the pedestrians disregarded the lights and crossed the street when they felt like it, figuring the lights to be only a suggestion for their walking patterns. Traffic struggled down the city streets. Earlier the snow had been cleared and packed against the curbs. But the snow continued to fall, and before long the streets would be blanketed and impassable again.

And where I stood, a mountain of the white stuff barricaded the corner. Mountain climbing wasn't on my agenda, but I climbed up and over the Alps, and made it across the street, cussing Steadwell all the way. I tried to do a good deed and offered to help an old lady navigate on the icy street, but she took one look at me and she clutched her purse to her chest and moved hurriedly away, feet spinning under her like a hamster on a treadmill. Well, peace on earth, good will to men and fuck her, too.

Prince's office was now within shouting distance—a good thing, because my trousers were as soggy as my disposition.

Chapter 6

Charlize's tits jiggled each time she laughed, and she laughed a lot. Me, I piled on the jokes just to watch them heave and sway. If me and her had to abandon some ship in the middle of the ocean, I'd pass up an inner tube any day, and hang tight to Charlize. Her flotation devices would carry us to China and back.

Charlize was a dyed-in-the-wool Harlem sister, in attitude and looks, with dreads wrapped up and banded in nation colors. She looked out of place planted among the conservative décor of Prince's office, but she was as sharp as, if not sharper than, Prince, a devil's chocolate of a woman, and though I suspected something besides salary bonded her to her employer, I carried on a light flirtation. Why not?

Banter with Charlize lightened my mood, and then, pleasantries aside, I deposited five hundred on the top of her desk, and she wrote me out a receipt. The sound of money landing must have touched off sensors in Prince's inner sanctum, because seconds after the money hit, he bounded through his door.

The phone rang at the same time. Charlize reached to answer the phone and Prince reached for the money. But Charlize saw him coming and was faster. She scooped up the money, stuffed it between Jell-O breasts, and answered the phone. What a woman.

Was it the money or Charlize's tits that Prince stared at? She ignored him, and we both checked ourselves while she completed the call, but I caught the dark expression on Prince's face. The tension in the air broke like brittle glass between them. I stepped out of the way. Hey, my name was Hess, wasn't in that mess.

"What are you doing?" Prince said to Charlize.

"What do you think?" Charlize snapped. She glared at him, and I swore the heat coming off her scorched the walls. I retired to a neutral corner and followed the action like I was at a tennis match. When it appeared that no more eruptions would take place, I coughed to remind them I was still in the room and said, "You two need anything else from me?"

Both their heads snapped in my direction. Prince recovered from his tizzy fit and pumped my hand. "Amos. Hey, fellow. Yes, come in, come in, why don't you. Let's chat."

Prince's well-cut suit hung on him magnificently, and he wore leather shoes that looked soft as butter. Business must be good, so what was up between him and Charlize?

"Uh, Prince, before I step inside your office I have to know you aren't charging me fifty bucks a minute for the pleasure."

Prince chuckled. "Aw, come on, Amos. What kind of business do you think I'm running?"

I eyed him. "Just let me know when I should bend over."

Prince turned, and like the spider and the fly, I followed Spider-Man through the door of his office and into his web.

Once inside, Prince flashed a deprecating smile. "Amos, we're friends—how can you think that?" A look from me told him not to push it, and he stopped the flimflamming.

Prince's office was laid out. Cash register sounds cha-chinged everywhere I looked. Big walnut desk, big stereo system, big wet bar, high-backed chairs that looked proper and uncomfortable, and rows upon rows of legal tomes that covered two walls. No sir, Prince wasn't doing bad at all. Well, listen and learn is what I always say. A woman's sweater was draped across a plush couch. Charlize's? And did the couch fold out to a bed?

Prince indicated one of the uncomfortable chairs. "Have a seat," he said. He pushed aside a stack of papers, offered me a cigar from his humidor, and sat in front of me perched on the edge of his desk. I declined the cigar and he said, "Have you heard?"

"Heard what?"

"Harry Bridges is dead. Heart attack. They found him an hour ago."

I stared at Prince and waited a moment, my mind going in ten directions at once. Finally I answered, "No shit." That seemed to be as good a comment as any. Huh, no poker game this week. Buster'll probably handle the funeral.

Prince raised his eyebrows, his face twitching and his freckles leaping across his nose like a moving giraffe as he talked. "Glad to see him go?"

Intrigued, I squinted at his moving freckles. "I cry at everybody's funeral," I said.

"Well, didn't you and Harry have a run-in a couple of years ago? And weren't you romantically involved with his niece, uh . . . what's her name?"

"Four years, but Harry and me came to an understanding. After which he left me the hell alone and I in turn didn't bother him."

"And his niece?" He leaned farther forward, his left eye twitching in a spastic wink.

Something rumbled inside my head, but I kept my expression neutral. *None ya' business, asshole.* Earlier, I had conjured up Catherine. And here Prince was talking about her. Coincidence? I folded my hands and stretched my long legs out in front of me.

"Let's talk about Steadwell," I said.

"Ah, yes. Steadwell. In a bit of trouble, isn't he?" he said.

"Might be if he were guilty, but he's not."

"Amos, that's what they all say."

Prince's smugness rubbed me the wrong way. Sure, I harbored doubts myself about whether Steadwell was completely innocent, but Prince's tone of voice still pissed me off. Then he snapped his fingers said, "Catherine—isn't that her name? Into the political scene, right? Yes, I often run into her from time to time. Still seeing her?"

He was as see-through as plastic wrap. I blanked on him. Poker had taught me some things. He waited and I let him wait. After he finally got it that I wasn't answering, he shrugged his shoulders, smiled, and said, "Steadwell. Right. Has he been arraigned?"

"Grand jury decided. It's murder two. Arraignment is tomorrow morning."

"You should have called sooner."

"I didn't know any sooner. Found out this morning after he'd been in jail a week. He's eighty, man. Can he get bail? Emotionally, he's losing it."

"After the first few days in jail, Steadwell didn't get a clue he was in serious trouble? He should have called a lawyer the minute he was arrested."

"Understand, Steadwell thinks he has bumpers on his ass and no one can rear-end him. He's lived a charmed life—never been arrested before, never been in jail, so he doesn't quite know how it works."

Prince considered. "That might work in his favor—if it's true that he has no record."

"It's the truth."

"I have to see him. But this weather . . . who knows when I can get to him?"

This time it was me that leaned forward. "Hey, the trains are running. Steadwell is old, man, don't you get it?"

Prince reared back and lifted an eyebrow. I raised him one better and lifted both of mine. He said, "Don't worry, Amos, I'll do my job."

Then he backtracked into our previous conversation as if we'd never left it. "You know, with Harry gone, Harlem is going to be wide open."

A rainbow of a smile spread across his face at the mention of Harry. "Wow. Drugs. Protection money. Think about it. Harlem's ripe, a veritable gold mine. Somebody's going to scoop up the action."

In my forty-two years on this earth, Prince was the only black man I'd ever heard of who said "wow" in just that way. His reaction to Harry's death troubled me. And the questions about Catherine? What was that about?

But I knew that if anybody could do anything for Steadwell, he could. He was a brilliant defense attorney whose star had risen in the past couple of years. He had made his bones by successfully defending two black brothers convicted of raping a Manhattan socialite, and in the course of the trial uncovered a sex scandal that involved the jet-setters and rocked Manhattan. Well-connected he was, and smart. Political elitists, on the white hand side, sponsored him unofficially. He was their boy.

Even so, a warning buzzed in my brain. I asked, "That something of interest to you?"

See, I played close to the chest—but Wow-man was primed—a big gush due out of him any second now, his eyes sparking like Christmas lights.

"No, no, not me, man. That's more up your alley—interested, Amos?"

"Harry's cousin Basil is taking over, last I heard. I'm not into that. My game is straight, has been for quite some time." I rose to go. "Look, maybe Steadwell'd be better off with another lawyer."

Prince vaulted off his desk as if someone had bit a chunk out of his ass. "Whoa, hold on, Amos. Don't be so touchy. Look, just checking—making sure, you know. I have to be careful with whom I have dealings."

He clamped my shoulder and hugged me so close I could smell what he had for lunch.

"Let me share something with you, Amos—"

I shifted my body away—what'd he think? I was some damn faggot? And he continued, "See, I'm going into politics—running for assemblyman, for starters. Harlem. What do you think?"

"Representing Harlem?" I geared my face down to neutral. Prince wasn't the public-servant type. "Huh. Well, I'd say, what you do with your life ain't none of my business."

"That's where you're wrong, Amos. Look here, if I do this, run for office, I'm going to need help—"

I interrupted. "Tapped out, man. Bought another brownstone, assets tied up, can't get money from me."

His eyes glinted and he said, "It's not money I need. You're well liked, Amos. You have influence now . . ."

I guffawed and Prince blinked, startled.

"I'm not kidding, Amos—I've asked around. You have more influence than you think. People high and low respect you. They don't call you the Harlem Don for nothing. An endorsement from a person like you, from the community, is what I need. Spread it around that you're in my corner."

There it was—that Harlem Don thing again.

"Seems to me, Prince," and I gestured to indicate his plush office, "you've pretty much deserted the community. Now you want to represent it?"

"I'm doing you a favor. I'm representing Steadwell, aren't I? And I'll get him off."

It didn't take a genius to get Prince's meaning. You grease me, I'll grease you.

"Let me see if I get it. You want me to pay you for representing Steadwell, and you want me to help you get elected, too? That's a pretty steep fee."

"Well, you know, Amos, my fees have gotten higher. Higher than most black folks can pay and what keeps me in business are my rich, white clients. I'm giving you and Steadwell a special rate because of our friendship."

I looked at him in disbelief. Prince was crazier than a loon. I headed for the door and said, "I'm outta here. Work on getting Steadwell out of jail."

Prince's harsh response stopped me cold. "One hand washes another, Amos," he said.

Blood shot to the top of my head. Almost dizzy, I spun around and in three steps strode back to where Prince stood and gave him the blackest look I could. Twelve years ago, it was me saved his yellow ass after Poontang Wanda had put a hit out on him. His face blotched red and obscured his freckles—he hadn't forgotten.

He stuttered, "What I meant to say—Steadwell's been accused of a capital crime. Only a miracle can get him out on bail."

"Well, Prince, I believe in miracles, don't you?"

Prince unbuttoned the collar on his shirt, sighed, and said, "Okay, okay, Amos, I'll try. But if I can't get to him before his arraignment, I'll get a bail application first thing and ask for a hearing. But let me warn you—bail, if I do get it, will be sky-high. You might have to put your property up, and there's no guarantee that even that'll be enough. Prepare yourself and Steadwell, too. Meanwhile, call this number." He turned back to his desk and thumbed through his Rolodex and handed me a card.

Babs' Bail Bonds, the card read. I tucked it into my pocket and said, "Steadwell is good people. He's been like a father to me. Do more than try, Prince."

Color flushed Prince's riney face. Our conversation over, I creased my lid, planted it on my head, and walked out of his office.

Prince tagged behind and said, "Wait, Amos, forgot to ask you— going to Harry's funeral?"

I flung over my shoulder, "Maybe."

In the reception area I turned. "Look, some advice—take it or leave it. If you're jumping into politics, better get real with an uptown office. Otherwise, what's the point?" That plugged him between the eyes. And made Charlize grin. I nodded to her and left.

On 72nd Street again, the dress shop called my name and I responded to its lure, a sucker on the line, caught as I entered the shop. Took no time at all. Moments later, I exited, carrying the scarlet dress, all boxed and gift wrapped.

Chapter 7

Two days later, I huddled, in a tee shirt and pajama bottoms, uncomfortable, stiff and freezing, on a chair in my bedroom in the early morning. A December chill had snaked into my apartment and lapped around my ankles. The brightly wrapped red-and-gold Christmas package stared at me from the corner. I had done nothing with it.

The pissing radiator informed me the heat was on, but the room was still frigid, no steam coming through. Pipes banged and clanked throughout the building to no avail. Seltzer, my pint-sized super, was in the basement working on the heater. I had been busy on the telephone this morning, but no plumber would come out in this weather, not on Sunday—and not to Harlem, a wonder that Seltzer had made it here.

Oscar, the sanitation worker who lived in the basement apartment, woke me up at five o'clock, complaining about the lack of heat. But then, Oscar always complained—about something, anything, or nothing—that was his nature. What the hell, I had gotten used to it.

I distributed electric heaters among the tenants in the building—only four apartments were occupied. The other four remained empty, and that was on purpose. Mostly I was satisfied with the folk I had around me, and didn't want to clutter the environment.

Winnie in one, Wilbur in another, me in another, and, of course, Oscar.

Oscar wasn't all bad, just a whiner, but I couldn't stand whiners. He had come up to the parlor floor and knocked on my door, practically in tears. I dispatched him quickly and jumped back in bed.

But six hours later, frost on my ass, I was shivering like a wimp myself, rocking back and forth in the chair. Deck the fucking halls . . .

Teeth chattering, I pounded on my chest to whip up courage as well as my blood. Then I jumped up and rummaged through the chest of drawers for a sweater and quickly pulled it over my head. I put on two pairs of socks and hoped that would be enough. Then I jerked the blankets off the bed and shrouded my entire body. Wrapped tight as a mummy, I sat down again and tried to get warm. My body temperature soon was restored to the temperature mammals are supposed to have and I threw off the blankets and dashed to put on the rest of my clothes while I could still move my limbs.

Outside my window, mounds of snow lay packed on the ground. Only the hardy would dare to venture outdoors today. Well, I guessed that meant me, 'cause here I was, going out in it. Had to. Rent to collect. The tenants were all snowed in, a perfect day to do it.

The house was quiet, except for the clanging in the basement. An added bonus of having only a few tenants. But Josephine was coming home tomorrow, so I had to get that damn heat going today. I'll find a damn plumber, if I have to drag him here myself.

Wilbur now lived in Patty's old apartment on the second floor because there was more room for him and Josephine. Took over Patty's daughter as well as her space, leaving his one-bedroom vacant.

So the whole top floor was now vacant. Zeke, the man who wanted me dead for his own perverted reason and who gave me genes and nothing else, died in his studio apartment. Murdered. The police never found his killer, but I knew who did it. Never rented out his room. Don't plan to.

Thinking about him soured my stomach. No way to start the day. Shit. I wrapped those gloomy thoughts in cobwebs, threw them over my shoulder, and proceeded to the kitchen to heat up some soup.

Hanging off the electric can opener, the can of chicken noodle soup chased itself merrily in a circle. I asked myself, *what kind of landlord doesn't want tenants?* And then I answered my own question. Somebody with sense.

By not renting my apartments out to the skeezers or deadbeats who daily knocked on my door looking for a place, I eliminated the mess and stress they always brought with them. Peace of mind is what I strove for nowadays, though it meant I was barely hanging on to the buildings. I needed the occasional bump from my poker winnings to keep my head above water.

Vigilant or not, a deadbeat always slipped under the radar. Two had recently infested my brownstone across the street, professional guests who had moved in six months ago, and so far, had never paid rent. Made four trips to Housing Court and only one tenant had been kicked out. The nigger got indignant when the Marshall showed up, said I couldn't kick him out of his own home. Made me laugh. Last time I heard, it was my name on the deed. Eighty-four-year-old Miss Ellie, a tenant and a former Cotton Club dancer, complained mightily about the new tenants' trashy ways and I didn't blame her.

Also, I had some unsavory types lodged in the newly purchased building that I couldn't get rid of, like the Honduran immigrant who fed me a sob story when he couldn't come up with the rent, but whom I later suspected dealt drugs out of his apartment. I locked his ass out and got in trouble with the HPD and he's right back in the apartment. I've taken notes, names and automobile license numbers, and handed the information over to the cops, but so far nothing. Needles and crack vials dotted the landscape around my new building. Lately, sleepless nights had been devoted to creative ways just short of extermination, to terminate his lease.

To be fair, most of my tenants were okay—good people who struggled every day, just like me, to hang tough in hard times, and who tried to make something of their community and their lives. Like Esther's kid, who got himself a full ride to Yale on a scholarship—not for his athleticism, but for his smarts, although truth be told, he could shoot some mean hoops.

And Jessie, the doctor, who stayed in my building while he was going to school—the whole neighborhood's proud of him—and only moved out because he got an internship somewhere in upstate New York. But he's lived all his life in Harlem and plans to return. Makes me mad when some outsider badmouths Harlem. I'm allowed, because I live here and love it. Same goes for those bougee black people who'd indulge in reveries of the glory days of Harlem, but wouldn't step their foot in Harlem today if you paid them. As if the Twenties were all Harlem was ever about.

A thunderous banging on my door stopped me mid-thought. Seltzer, my super, streamed into the room, spewing like a volcano, cussing, sputtering, and spitting.

"Need parts—damn it all. Got to replace a pipe. What the hell you doing? Taking a vacation? Is we going to fix the heater or not?"

"What the hell—listen, just 'cause you got keys to my place don't mean you can bust in here anytime you feel like it. I've called for a plumber. Nobody's responded. Plumbers are the ones on vacation, not me."

"You call Shoo-Fly Smith?"

"Hell no, Seltzer, and don't even bring his nasty name up. Ain't calling Shoo-Fly. He's not even a bonafide plumber."

"He the onliest one have parts and come out in this weather. Call him."

I wrinkled my nose in distaste. "Who's the boss here, negro? Your friend Shoo-Fly is nothing but a garbage dump that flies chase after. You need a gas mask to be in the same room with him. Am I right or am I right?"

"You got a better suggestion?"

A knock on the door interrupted. Everybody in the building disregarded my Do-Not-Disturb-Outside-of-Office-Hours sign. Why I had the fool thing up I don't know. Nobody paid it the least bit of attention.

"Come in," I shouted.

Winnie, a postal employee who lived in the second floor front, poked her round face through the doorway, the fragrance of fresh-baked bread wafting behind her.

Me, I appreciated Winnie, but a lot of men couldn't get past the fact that Winnie was an ample woman and nearly six feet tall. Still—she had curves that ran down her body like a well-tended highway. You could seek comfort, if you wanted, on the pillows of Winnie's chest or delight in holding on to a bowling ball of a rump that quivered with each strut of her powerful legs. And Winnie's dimples, her best feature, were deeply plowed ravines in a wide, agreeable, espresso-coffee face. Her dimples reminded me of Catherine's. Why, if Winnie weren't a tenant, I might . . . Never mind, I dismissed the thought before it had time to settle. Made it a rule never to mix business with pleasure, and I stuck with it.

Worry lines stood out on Winnie's forehead as she stepped across my threshold and handed me a fresh loaf of banana nut bread, still warm from the oven, and without preamble said, "Patty's back, Mr. Brown. I seen her."

I froze mid-loaf. "You've seen her? Here? Wilbur's seen her, too."

"No. Greg's Fish and Rib Joint. Dropped off two coconut cakes for Greg yesterday, and seen her. She tell me—eyes all wide and crazy—she gone come and get her daughter."

Winnie baked on the side for local restaurants and a few greasy spoons in the area, so it made sense that she had bumped into Patty in one of them.

"Same thing Wilbur said," I replied.

Seltzer picked at a callus on his hand and said, "A damn shame—leaving her kid like that—"

Winnie nodded in agreement. "Umph, umph, umph. Ain't that the truth. And now, of all times, like a bad penny, she turns up. It sure ain't the proper time to be worrying Wilbur. He carrying enough of a burden."

"You mean with Josephine?" I said.

A puzzled look crested on Winnie's face and her eyes darted back and forth between Seltzer and me. A soul-deep sadness spilled from her eyes and she shook her head, "No, Mr. Brown—that's the least of his troubles . . . Mr. Brown, Wilbur's sick—ain't you noticed?"

I knitted my brows together. What was she talking about?

Winnie said, "He ain't himself. Same thing happening to him like what happened to Scotty Two Shoes. Remember him?"

Scotty Two Shoes had been the neighborhood's cross-dresser, and had tipped around Harlem for years in pumps and frilly dresses. "Died a year ago of pneumonia, didn't he? What's that got to do with Wilbur?"

Seltzer butted in, "Lots of people dying around here, ain't you noticed? It ain't ammonia, either." He rolled his eyes at me and nodded to Winnie.

"Seltzer, you dumb as Balaam's ox. Pneumonia, fool, pneumonia." Seltzer and I both liked ragging on each other and we did it on a regular basis. Today was no different.

"New, old—don't make no difference when you sick."

"What are you suggesting?"

Winnie said, "Now don't get upset, Mr. Brown—"

Seltzer slid his thumb and forefinger up and down his bubble of a nose like a trombone and finally blurted, "You the dummy. Damn fool—can't see nothing 'til it bites you in the ass."

"Across a poker table, I can see a gnat's wing drop. Ain't nothing wrong with my eyesight."

"I'm talking people, fool. You can't see nothing when it comes to people. Now, what I think, I'd bet Wilbur's come down with that homo cancer."

"What homo cancer?" I looked at the both of them like they had lost their minds.

"Mr. Brown," Winnie said, her voice faltering, "I love Wilbur like he was my brother. We been neighbors for over twenty years. I—I'm just scared for him. I tried to get him to talk to me, but he won't. He really don't look well and he won't say nothing about what's going on with him. I know about that sickness. It was me helped take care of Two Shoes when he was failing, and I seen the marks. Wilbur's got those same kinds of marks. He's tried to cover them up with makeup, but I seen them." Winnie hung her head so low it rested on her ample bosom.

Seltzer added, "Who you think been helping him carry his groceries up the steps? You? I don't think so. You too busy to see the man is weak, and getting weaker."

I stared, reeling from their news.

All this time I had been concerned about Josephine, never realizing that anything was the matter with Wilbur.

"Yep, you got to be pretty stupid not to notice something like that," Seltzer said.

Seltzer, the little shit, was like a dog with a bone—he wouldn't give up on it, and he wasn't subtle. Remorse gnawed at me. How could I have missed what was happening with Wilbur? The new cancer—rumor or fact? I never thought Wilbur as one of *those* people—not really. I mean, he was Wilbur, for chrissakes. Why hadn't he said something?

"Winnie, are you sure?"

"Mr. Brown, believe me. Wilbur got the sickness. And he ain't the only one. People at my job—one day they at work, next day you don't see them."

We looked at each other. The news about Wilbur affected us all, but right now I felt as if I personally owned the pain.

"Before the rumors start, let me clear this up with Wilbur. Don't say nothing to nobody."

"Oh, you can trust us. But you know how people is, Mr. Brown. A body's business ain't their own in Harlem town 'cause everybody know it. People already avoiding him. Say he got the plague."

"Well, we won't contribute to their paranoia, okay?"

Winnie bobbed her head. "That's right, Mr. Brown. You can count on me." As she left the apartment she added, "Poor Josephine."

Speechless, I stared at Winnie's departing figure.

Seltzer pulled his cap over his head and cleared his throat. "Wilbur all right with me. I help him. I don't listen to nobody."

"Glad you admit you don't listen to anybody." One last shot—I couldn't help it.

"You a damn fool," Seltzer said, and he left, too.

To a closed door and empty air I said, "Thanks for the bread."

*　*　*

Each step up the stairs to Wilbur's apartment felt as if I were walking the last mile. It was evening when I knocked on his door. Upset when he didn't answer my knock, I used my keys and stepped inside his apartment. No one there. The place was neat and tidy as usual. Only a few toys lay about. Of course. Wilbur must still be at the hospital.

I realized right away how much I didn't want to have this conversation. I was relieved at not finding him there. Was this my business? Wilbur hadn't asked for any help, and it was obvious he wanted to keep this personal challenge private.

Feeling guilty about invading his space, I quickly got out of there and locked his door behind me. Tomorrow was another day. I'd talk to him tomorrow.

I returned to my own apartment. My body felt like someone had hammered on my back and shoulders. Tomorrow. Tomorrow was also Steadwell's hearing. I sank into my bed and groaned aloud in sweet relief, the bed felt so good. I cocooned underneath the covers. Another day, tomorrow. I sighed and slipped off into sleep.

Heavy feet walked across my chest and I stirred. The pressure suffocated me. My chest pounded. It was Wilbur's footsteps, thumping across my chest, up one flight of stairs, then all the way to heaven.

Chapter 8

The courtroom looked like Grand Central at rush hour. I took a seat in the back, hoping I wasn't making a fat mistake. A low-level hum circulated throughout the room. Lawyers in dark suits buzzed and lit like flies on and around the tables in front of the judge's bench. Guards walked back and forth, their eyes drifting over the assembled onlookers and then back to the activity at the front of the room. A court reporter sat, solemn and bored with glazed-over eyes.

Prince sat on the first row of benches along with two other attorneys. He leaned on the wooden railing in front of him and looked back to share a joke with them, his manner easy, relaxed and assured. The attorneys guffawed at his joke, indifferent to the miseries of the people playing out in front of them. The judge looked up at the laughter, frowned, and then resumed her reading.

Prince, at thirty-four, was eight years younger than me. Like me, he made a big mistake early on. He tried to straddle two continents, but he wasn't Atlas. Attempts at a penny-ante protection racket in his early twenties didn't pay off, so in order to finance his last two years at Harvard, he tried extortion and Wanda Plessant was his mark.

"Poontang Wanda," they called her, a woman who operated a friendly whorehouse off 139th Street in Harlem for over twenty years and was in business to this day. An upstart back then, Prince didn't know his ass from a hole in the ground. Dipping his wick in Wanda's business pissed her off big-time. And Poontang Wanda didn't take it lying down—the old girl responded, made some calls, and put a hit out on him.

Me, I heard about the hit through the Harlem grapevine, and interceded. Seemed lunacy to me to have all that education washed, like dirt, down a drain. I respected education, envied those that had it. The United Negro College Fund's dictum—"A mind is a terrible thing to waste" made fucking sense to me.

Scared shitless, Prince came to recognize the error of his ways. Since me and Wanda was friends, I went to her and explained the situation. I told her Prince's back was up against a wall, which made him do rash things. The devil made him do it, so to speak. She relented on the hit, and get this, even coughed up the money to pay for his last two years of school.

When I brought him the news, instead of being grateful, the fool thought he had gotten over on Wanda. We had a consultation and I busted his lip. He saw the light pretty quick after that and came to his senses. Like I said—smart. Wanda wasn't no dummy, either. Bought herself a lawyer for life. And look at him now.

Steadwell's name and docket number was called. Prince's turn up and he strutted to center stage. Two officers brought Steadwell in. I gasped at the sight. Steadwell looked ready to keel over.

Ready for the windup and pitch, Prince smiled at the judge, but she didn't return the smile. When he opened his mouth to speak, she interrupted him right away.

"I don't know what we're here for, Counselor—this matter has already been heard. Your client has been remanded on a charge of second-degree murder. Unless you're going to show me some new steps, my dance card is already booked, and I don't need to go through this again."

"But Your Honor, at the time of my client's indictment, Mr. Steadwell wasn't represented by present counsel, and I believe he was given short shift on a trumped-up charge."

She raised an eyebrow. "Trumped-up charge? I don't have time for this. You can argue the merits of this case at trial. Until then—"

"I know that, Judge Stevens, and we're preparing for trial, but until that time—look here, my client is ill, has been ill for quite some time. I have a doctor's statement to that effect. May I approach?"

The judge nodded, and regarded Steadwell, who had bent over so far forward in his seat that his nose practically touched the table in front of him. "Regrettably, his health was a non-issue at the grand jury trial and that's unfortunate. To think that my client is capable of overpowering a victim and stabbing him five times is patently ridiculous. Since his incarceration, he's become successively weaker. The truth is, Judge—" and here Prince paused for effect, "he may not last until his trial. The man is eighty-three years old." The weight of Prince's hand on Steadwell's shoulder bent him another inch closer to the table.

Jesus, Steadwell was older than I thought.

Prince continued. "He's not a risk for flight, anyone can see that. He's been at the same address for over sixty years. Judge, if he weren't black, this man never would have been charged."

At that, the judge held up her hand. "I don't want to hear it, Counselor—"

"Surely, Your Honor can make accommodations for his present health, and order a reasonable bail set for this man."

Steadwell slumped lower over the table seat while the judge eyeballed him. Then she said, "D.A.'s office got anything to say? Mr. Corwell?"

A potbellied ADA, who looked to be no older than thirty, if that, and who possessed a pudgy face on which rested a pair of wire-rimmed glasses, jumped to his feet and piped, "As your honor has already said, the State has been through this. The accused has been charged with murder two because he viciously, and with malice, stabbed and killed a defenseless man for the most baseless reason—because his victim stole the accused's stolen mink coats."

The judge frowned. "Come again?" She looked back at Steadwell, his face inches off the table. "Skip it. How old was the victim?"

"How old? Uh—one minute, Your Honor, I'll tell you," ADA Corwell said while he shuffled through a bunch of papers. The judge tapped her pen impatiently. One minute stretched to two, then three. The judge picked up a newspaper to read.

"Uh, thirty-one, your honor."

The judge put down the paper and blew a raspberry from Her Honor's lips. "Bail is set at one hundred thousand, cash or bond. Because of the defendant's health, we're going to do this quick. I'm assuming there'll be no objection from the defense. The trial date will be set for next month." She nodded to her Clerk, "Find a date. Next case."

"But—" Attorney Corwell said.

The judge slammed down her gavel. "You didn't hear me? Next case, I said."

I sighed in relief. Steadwell collapsed still further, his nose mashed against the table and drool sliding out of his mouth. Prince set him upright and tried to lift him to his feet. In a few strides I reached the two of them and assisted. Steadwell smiled a pitiful smile, and I pumped Prince's hand.

He said, "We got lucky. The bail is low because the judge is on our side. This case is a slam dunk. A good thing, because there's not much time to prepare." He pointed me in the direction of the bail clerk, and he hurried from the courtroom.

Babs' Bail Bonds had taken care of me earlier, and I finished the business with the clerk and returned to where Steadwell stood and clapped him gingerly on the shoulder. He faltered a little. "I'll wait while you, uh, check out," I said.

Huh. Six hours later I had wilted from the wait, but Steadwell emerged from Central Booking fresh as a spring salad, his step spry and brisk, no indication of the declining octogenarian I had seen in the courtroom.

Sly old fox. I shoulda known.

Chapter 9

The following day I sat in my office, writing out bills. I rubbed my hands together, fingers frozen stiff and hard to bend, the air in the room colder indoors than out. The heater beside the desk whirred and popped, but so far had not produced enough heat to warm a cockroach. Day three—no plumber and no heat. The steam had come on for only a day after Shoo-Fly had worked on it. Using these electric heaters, my Con Ed bill would be sky-high.

I picked up an envelope. What do you know? Another bill. I stashed it and the rest of the bills beneath the blotter and closed the checkbook. Five years ago a checking account wasn't something I'd have considered. Like any brother working the street, I'd always dealt in cash money.

Huh. I exhaled a mighty gust and the blotter flapped its wings, ready for takeoff. The bills made a fulcrum and the blotter tottered over it. I shuffled paper and the bills peeked past the edges of the blotter like lettuce and formed a finance sandwich.

Had my decision to purchase another brownstone been wise? Times like these I wondered. Not having money made me nervous. Time for poker? Did I need to search out a game? Since my breakup with Catherine, my playing had escalated and I knew I had to cool it. People depended upon me now. Luck doesn't last forever and no one knew that better than me.

The law of averages said I was due for a loss, but knowing that didn't stop the itch.

I paced the room, stopping every so often to listen to life going on in the building. Upstairs voices told Dolly it was nice to have her back where she belonged. Wilbur and his show tunes. After he had picked up Josephine from the hospital we spoke briefly, but I couldn't bring up his condition, especially in front of Josie.

I got a hard look at him, though, and saw what Winnie saw. He looked emaciated, and the makeup couldn't hide the lesions on his face. He waved bony hands in the air without his usual vivacity, and his processed hair, Wilbur's supreme conceit, hung about his shoulders, lusterless and lank.

I walked over to one of the twenty foot windows that fronted my office and thought, a quick game couldn't hurt—play a couple of hours. Snow glistened in the morning light, blindingly beautiful, perfect and pristine. Why couldn't life be that way? Why couldn't I be that way?

Then, without notice, a dark hyphen gloomed across my line of vision. A hearse moved through the expanse of whiteness and a chill snaked down my spine. I jumped back from the window. Sweat dotted my forehead.

A funeral, fool—that's all it is—somebody's funeral. There was, after all, a church on the corner. Still, I felt uneasy. A message had been delivered—Western Union style—and I had panicked. My old man, Zeke the Freak, was laughing in his grave. Him with his black magick and his visions would get a kick out of my reaction. I plopped back into my swivel chair. Good thing I wasn't superstitious. If I were—

I rapped the wooden desk three times. A shaft of air blew past my neck, cold as a popsicle, and I jumped again. I knew it. Something awful was about to happen.

Where in the fuck was Steadwell?

Wilbur and Steadwell both on my mind, both in trouble, so my imagination was working overtime, that was all.

But Steadwell hadn't answered his phone yesterday, nor the day before. I succumbed to a premonition and picked up the phone and dialed his number, my fingers stiff from the cold, my hand a frozen monkey paw. Checking, that's all, making sure the old man was okay.

The phone rang endlessly. I gnawed on my bottom lip. The old trickster was probably out on the streets doing business. I let it ring a few more times before I finally hung up.

Agitated now, I rose and paced. A junkie zigzagged through the snow beneath my window. I watched his progress and matched my thoughts to his movement. When he zigged to the right, I thought of Wilbur and his situation. When he zagged to the left, I thought of Steadwell. The telephone rang and, in a wink, after I picked up the receiver, all thoughts were suspended as I heard the soft drizzle of a female voice melting like butter in my ear.

"Amos?"

"Yeah?"

"It's Catherine."

I paused. "Yeah, I know. I still recognize your voice."

Another silence from her end, then . . .

"You heard about Uncle Harry?"

"Yeah—sorry. Harry was . . . okay—in his way."

"Mama wanted me to call you. Tell you about the funeral. Eleven o'clock Saturday. Can you come?"

Her Momma suggested she call, huh? I cleared my throat and said, "Give your mother my condolences, will you? Of course I'll be there. Uh—do you need anything?"

"Amos?"

"What?"

Another pause on the line. "Never mind," Catherine said. "I'll see you Saturday."

After she hung up I stared at the receiver and thought how she would look in the dress I bought her. I imagined the expression on her face, and it put a lump in my throat. Then the movie playing in my head fast-forwarded to Catherine with the dress off, and that put a lump inside my pants. Damn.

Buzz-hiccup. Buzz-hiccup. Hang the damn phone up. I replaced the receiver and the noise stopped.

Why did this woman get under my skin? Since our breakup I hadn't lacked for female companionship, but the affairs had been short, sweet, and impermanent—kind of how I wanted it. Additional thoughts of Catherine skittered through my brain. I've tried to close the book on that relationship, but the pages kept falling open. Harlem's too small and I kept running into her. Saw her from a distance at Wilt's Club, and another time up close at a community meeting at Abbysinian Baptist Church. I singed myself from a spark I caught off her, but we merely said hello, nothing more. I could have said something. Why didn't I?

Like Seltzer said, "You're a damn fool, Amos Brown."

Back to the real world. I snatched the phone again, dialed a florist, and ordered a wreath for Harry's funeral. Now, to kill two birds with one stone—I'd drop by the gym and then check on Steadwell. I locked the office door for privacy, went to the closet, stooped to take money from the floor safe, divided the cash in half, banded it, and stuffed it in my hip pocket.

No sooner had I come out of the closet—an ugly thought—than a symphony sounded in the basement. Seltzer in the cellar. Boff-clang. Boff-clang. Dum-de-dum-de-dum-dum—I knew that tune. I put on my cold-weather gear and made my way below.

Seltzer was huffing and blowing—the usual for him—and nuts, bolts, and pipes lay scattered before him on the wet cement floor.

I leaned against a dank wall. "Think you can get the heater going again?" I said.

"It's going."

"Shoo-Fly didn't fix it."

"Did. This here's another leak."

I sighed. "Fuck it. Blow the damn thing up."

"Can't. You can't afford another one."

"Got that right. So can you fix it?"

"Ya damn fool. Didn't I just say I could?"

I smiled and turned to go, leaving Seltzer to perform his magic. "Don't know what I'd do without you, Seltz—"

"Me neither. Give me another raise."

"Like you said—can't afford it."

Selzter's nose twitched like a rabbit and his lips split into a grin. Another game we played. Him asking for a raise, and me refusing. I nodded and left him playing with his pipes.

Outside, the sun was shining, but it was still a cool blue morning. Icicles melted off trees and dripped on me as I trudged in the direction of the Police Athletic League's gym in Harlem. The money burned a hole in my pocket. Tempting me. An itch that needed scratching. No. I kept my feet moving in the right direction and puffed like a steam engine, not an easy walk through this snow. Yet I was making better progress than if I'd driven. Besides, I figured I needed the exercise. And parking was bad around Steadwell's place.

A Hallmark greeting card scene played out in front of me. Children bounced snowballs off each other's heads, and tumbled and flailed in the snow. One boy had rigged a wooden crate with curtain rods attached, and pushed his own one-horse open sleigh up a slight incline. Then he jumped in and waited for the crate to move downhill. It did—but very slowly. Given the crate's mph, I figured he ought to reach the end of the block by Christmas next year, but his face was lit like a star and he was proud of his contraption. Pure happiness shot out of him, and wasn't that the point of it all?

I reached my destination, a drab building constructed in the last century, and climbed the stairs to the boxing gym on the second floor. Opening the door, noise and funk greeted me.

I surveyed the room and found who I was looking for—a beer-barreled white man with a red Irish face. He was screaming at a spindly black youth in blue-gray shorts whose arms were weighted down with gargantuan boxing gloves too heavy and too big for his small frame.

I made my way toward the pair, past a boxing ring where two young pugilists roundhoused each other with more gusto than aim, more misses than hits.

Sergeant McGillihand's robust personality shepherded this youth program; his was a torrent of energy that could devastate as well as defend. Feeling the onslaught of his wrath, the youth stood defense-less and mute, head hanging low and lower lip trembling. When McGillihand spotted me, the steam subsided. He gestured the boy away and ordered him back to the bag. "And I want to see effort," he added.

The boy, twelve or thirteen years old, scooted off, happy to escape. I raised my eyebrows at McGillihand. "Little rough, weren't you?"

The beet-red of McGillihand's face shifted back to its normal pink color and he said, "Not rough enough. Hanging with the wrong element, he's missed a week of practice. Hammered his butt in front of a crack house and dragged him back here. He's smart—I'm not losing him—here is where he belongs."

I nodded, and looked over to where the boy was pounding out his feelings on a bag. I'd been there. Inside the musty gym, I counted fifteen others doing the same thing, working out ghetto angst with their small fists. A few boys skipped and jumped rope. Two of the youngest ones chased each other in circles around the room. One glare from McGillihand stopped them, and they duti-fully returned to their job of lifting weights.

MGillihand looked out for his kids—they were fortunate to have somebody like him watch their backs. Hey, if I'd had somebody, maybe I wouldn't have landed my butt in an adult reformatory at sixteen. Well, that was the past—water over the dam, or under the moat or something like that . . .

I pulled money from my pocket and handed it over to McGillihand. No words. This was a routine. He slipped it into his pants pocket. "Always need more equipment. Happy to take guilt money." He paused, "One of these days, Amos, you're going to lose."

I shrugged. "McGillihand, I lose all the time. I show up here when I win."

"Ought to give the gambling up."

I indicated the room. "Tell them that."

He nodded and we watched the kids work out for a few minutes before I said, "By the way, how're they doing?"

"School grades good. Ten kids vying for championships—different levels. Sammy over there—about to turn pro. No one's giving me grief this year, and that's a first—except boneheaded Robbie." Robbie was the kid he had just dressed down.

"He'll come around—like the others. Patience, ain't that the ticket?"

"Sometimes cracking heads helps. Robbie is two inches from a head cracking."

McGillihand blustered, but he wasn't fooling me. I thumped his shoulder. "Okay, McGillihand—rolling on—"

"All right. Look here, the big tournament's after Christmas. We going to see you?"

"Sure," I said. And for no other reason but because I was there, I asked him, "Say, you heard about Dap Jones, didn't you? You know what went down?"

"Dap?" McGillihand squeezed his bushy eyebrows together until they met in a line in the middle of his forehead. "Robert Jones, you mean? He used to be one of mine. Turned into a punk-ass pimp."

I shrugged my shoulders. "Well, shit, McGillihand, you can't save everybody. It ain't your fault."

He glared at me, and his face did it again, turned red as a brick and he snorted his disgust. "Even when Robert was a kid—always trying to get over on somebody. Probably deserved what he got. Heard the 28th got the perp."

"Yeah. Deacon Steadwell—know him?"

McGillihand shook his head.

"He's a friend of mine—I'm thinking he didn't do it."

McGillihand snorted again and said, "The hell you say. Sure he did it. Took three cops to bring him down."

I narrowed my eyes. "Three? Deacon Steadwell is eighty-three years old. How's that possible?"

"You asked—I'm telling you—that's what I heard. Pissed off my friends big-time."

"Personal friends?" I frowned.

McGillihand lifted his shoulders. "They're blue, so they're my friends, know what I'm saying?"

I knew. If Steadwell gave the arresting cops trouble, a good enough excuse to pin a rap on him. I shook McGillihand's hand and left the gym, heading for Steadwell's. No more lollygagging.

Chapter 10

Ibuzzed the apartment. No answer, of course, and the front door to his building, locked solid. No way to get in, unless I snuck myself in as somebody came out. Okay, that plan would have to do. I hung around the entrance for a few minutes and sure enough, luck. In the form of a young sister, probably in her early twenties, with owl eyes and thick glasses, who dashed out of the front door, a book bag strapped on her back. She came through so fast I barely caught the door before it closed. And then, on a hummer, I asked her. "Say, you happen to know Deacon Steadwell?" I said, holding the door open.

She suspiciously eyed both me and the door. "Why you asking?"

A fair question, and one I'd certainly ask any stranger invading my building. "I'm a friend of his. Haven't seen him for a few days and I'm worried about him. He's an old man, you know."

Her eyes flitted back and forth like fireflies and she exhaled coffee breath through tight lips. Uh-oh. What did that reaction mean?

"Saw him day before yesterday. Haven'tseenhimtoday," she said in a whoosh.

I waited. "Anything else?"

She hesitated, her young face looked troubled and her owl eyes blinked wide behind the glasses.

"It's okay. You can trust me—really. I helped get him out of jail."
I paused. "Or maybe you didn't know he'd been in jail?"

"Yeah, I knew. I live across the hall from him. You creeped me
out when you asked about him. Like, how did you know? Last time
I saw him he wasn't right."

"What do you mean, he wasn't right?"

"Screaming, he was, inside his apartment."

"When exactly did you see him?"

"Yesterday morning. I heard him as I was about to leave my
apartment—I go to City College. Knocked on his door to see if he
was okay. Mr. Steadwell's a nice man."

"And was he okay?"

She shook her head. "Hell, no. Said he was going to kill him
somebody. Waved a gun around and scared the shit out of me, and
then he ran off. Didn't even lock his door. That's the last I saw of
him."

This wasn't good. I pulled a business card from my wallet and
gave it to her and said, "Look, if he comes back, if you see him, give
me a call?"

She stared at the card and then stuck it inside her book bag.
"Ain't going to be here for a coupla days. Studying with a friend.
But when I come back, if I see him—then sure, I'll call you."

"You think his door is unlocked now?"

"No, turned the inside latch and shut it. It's locked."

A good neighbor. What the hell. I let the door swing to, thanked
her, and she hurried off. Worried, I hung on the steps for a minute,
thinking. Then I headed home. I passed vendors in the freezing
cold, hawking evergreen trees and Christmas wreaths. I picked up a
tree. Two days until Christmas. And then, since I was so near . . .

Let me make one more stop.

The late Harry the Monkey Chaser's old office-slash-pool hall
was only two blocks away and it was one of Steadwell's old hang-
outs. Maybe he'd been around—or maybe somebody there might
know where to find him.

*   *   *

Smoke hung like a mournful cloud over the straggle of people at Harry's place. A pool player chalked his cue and stalked the table, while his competitor leaned, foot against wall, holding his stick, and thoughtfully watched the action.

Tree in hand, I bumped shoulders and touched knuckles with a few of the bloods, and made inquiries about Steadwell. They laughed at my tree, but nobody admitted to seeing Steadwell. From a dark corner, hooded eyes observed me and after a few minutes signaled me over. I went, dragging the tree behind me.

Basil, the late Harry the Monkey Chaser's first lieutenant and successor to Harry's throne, smiled at my approach. Basil was a tall West Indian brother and, like everybody that worked for Harry, his relative. Second cousin, I think. But Basil had no trace of a lilt in his speech. He had broad shoulders and a granite face and was smoother than 600-count sheets. He came off as more refined than Harry had ever been, but make no mistake, he was a treacherous S.O.B. He sucked on a cigarillo and looked me up and down. His glance ended at the tree I was carrying.

Basil made a fluid gesture and indicated I should sit, so I did and laid the tree next to me on the floor. "Damn, man, your pine needles are shedding," he said.

I shrugged. "The needles will improve the smell in here."

"Funny. A drink, Amos?"

The man was stylish—all coat and tie and well-cut suit. Graceful, too, yet he frightened most men—no one wanted to mess with Basil, including me. Basil had notches on his gun and menace in his heart.

"Naw, Basil—too early for a drink. Heard about Harry. Sad."

Basil scowled and puffed on his cigarillo. Smoke rings, like halos, floated above his head. What was wrong with that picture? "You coming to Harry's funeral?"

"Planning on it. Why?"

"In case of trouble, wanted to know whose side you're on."

"At Harry's funeral? You think there'll be trouble? C'mon, Basil—who'd pull some shit like that?"

"Stupid people. Greedy people. Taking inventory—need to know where loyalties lie. Your invitation to the funeral might be rescinded."

"Catherine invited me."

"Ah, yes, still together? Good. Makes no difference." A hint of a smile played behind Basil's lips, but there was a threat behind his easy speech.

Seemed like Basil was waiting for me to wilt like a pansy, so putting him straight seemed the right thing to do. Still, underneath my jacket pinpricks of sweat dotted the back of my shirt.

"Look, Basil—I told Harry before, and I'm telling you—I'm not a part of your drug scene. Consider me Switzerland. I have no alliances. Make no mistake, I'd like to see the drugs leave Harlem. But I know that's not going to happen anytime soon. You're taking over for Harry, I get it. More power to you. I just hope you continue to honor the agreement that me and Harry had. My block is off-limits. I'm hoping you won't change that."

A drift of smoke curled about Basil's face. "Everything changes. It's the nature of things. Some things you can't control."

"And some things you can," I said.

"Man, listen, got my men out in full force. Harry is dead and people are scrambling for the spoils. I'm overextended. Tell you what, though, to keep your block intact, I think you ought to pay for the privilege, see what I'm saying? Way things are going, you and your block both might be in jeopardy. Who can tell? Keep on the right side of the action and chances are you might not get hurt."

Basil tapped the ash from his baby cigar into an ashtray, took a hit and the smoke blew into my face. The man was straight-out asking for protection money. I didn't respond. Would Basil notice?

Basil continued, "Harry's dead. In a couple of years, I may be moving on—past Harlem, got bigger fish to fry. But for now . . ."

"But for now? You want me under your thumb, is that it? Basil, what you don't understand is that I ain't in the life no more, don't plan to step back in it, so there's no point to handling me." I rose and reached for the tree, hoping Basil wouldn't notice my shaking hand, stood the tree upright and looked Basil in the eye.

Never let anyone bully you, that was my motto, or you'd never be finished with the bull or the bullies. Me, I was full of gall and more than happy to share some of it with Basil. "What you do with

your business is *your* business. I'm out of it. See you at Harry's funeral, Basil."

"There'll be only one Don in Harlem."

"Sure, Basil," I said. "I ain't competing—got no problem."
Dragging my tree behind me, I bid Basil good-bye and headed out
the door. At the entrance, I sneaked a covert look back. Basil ground
the cigarillo between his teeth, took a puff and it flamed an angry
red.

Chapter 11

The night before Christmas and all through the house . . .

In the early evening hours at the brownstone Winnie was cooking up a storm in her apartment. So was Wilbur. For our traditional Christmas dinner—which began when I took over as landlord for the building—I had gotten up early and purchased the dinner fixings at a supermarket over in Jersey. Lots of fresh food choices in Jersey—couldn't say the same about Harlem. Harlem residents had to travel outside their community if they wanted quality. And that went for more than food. Someday . . .

The whole building smelled of cinnamon and spices, baking bread, roasted turkey, and other tantalizing aromas. Made me want to holler, it smelled so good. Hard to wait until tomorrow, but the wait would be worth it and the event was something everybody looked forward to. Of course, anything was better than a meal out of a can and, for me, that was the alternative.

Yesterday I dropped off the Christmas tree to Wilbur. Unlike me, he knew what to do with it when it came to decorating. Since Wilbur's disability check hardly covered his and Josephine's expenses each month, the tree seemed to be a treat for both of them.

I hadn't yet broached the subject of his illness. Never the right time to bring it up. Anyway, the last few days Wilbur looked almost like his old self, and I didn't want to mess with that.

"Jingle Bell Rock" and sounds of static jangled merrily together out of the radio on Wilbur's kitchen counter. When I popped in he was prancing around the Christmas tree in his chartreuse smoking jacket in time with the beat. Good to see that. I set a bottle of 151 rum next to the radio and poured Wilbur and myself a drink.

Though Wilbur never mentioned it, he was semi-famous. Danced on the Broadway stage, a member of the original cast of *The Wiz*—but a fall three years ago bounced him from the cast and wiped out his career. A shame. Harlemites took pride in that show, even if they never got to see it because they knew it was filled with a whole lot of black people and that was reason enough for them. Me, I saw the show—must have even seen Wilbur perform, but who could tell with those costumes? One flying monkey pretty much looked like any other.

His scrapbook was pretty impressive—he'd danced in quite a few shows. Yet the living room wall of his apartment was decorated with only a single Wiz production photo. Wilbur and six other dancers posed in the wall picture, outfitted in their flying monkey suits. A symbol of his success or a bitter reminder? Whatever, it was unfortunate that his life seemed to be distilled to a single photo.

I sipped my drink and looked at monkeys while Wilbur and Josephine put the finishing touches on the tree. Josie bubbled over with the excitement of Christmas and spun around the room like a dervish. A princess in cockamamie pink, a tiara dangling off the side of her head, she whirled and twirled and tripped over herself. Both Wilbur and I lunged to catch her and slammed into one another. "Watch it, Josephine," Wilbur shouted. Josephine righted herself and looked at us like we were the fools, as indeed we were. She giggled. I empathized with Wilbur. He had said it before—Josephine was precious, but she was also a ticking bomb.

Covering his distress, Wilbur told Josephine, "Quit running. Fluff yourself up. Slow down and show Mr. Brown how you can walk like a model. Go 'head, girl. Give him the style and dip."

Josephine, ready for the new game, adjusted the dangling tiara and sashayed the length of the room, hands on hips, pelvis pushed forward. At the end of the room she dipped low, pivoted, and turned.

Wilbur clapped happy hands. "Work it, child, work it. Now fling that hair." He demonstrated and snapped his head around and his processed locks slapped him in the face. Ouch. Then he froze, lips pouty, in a sexy pose.

Josephine mimicked him. She snapped her head the way Wilbur showed her and her barrettes popped her in the face and stung her cheeks. Double ouch. For a second she looked about ready to cry, but Wilbur distracted her with his cheerleading.

"Ah-ah-ah. What price beauty, child. What price beauty. No, no, no—keep going, girl, strut on."

According to the gospel of Wilbur, pain was but a small price to pay for beauty. I shook my head. "Wilbur, you ought to be ashamed, teaching that child that nonsense."

"Now, Mr. B., every woman knows you got to go through pain to have beauty. Being a man, you wouldn't know nothing about that, but I do. Any woman who's faced the straightening comb, a jugs-up bra, high-heel shoes, or a girdle will tell you what I'm talking about. Come here, Josie, let me give you Life Lesson Number One."

I gnawed at my lip. Should I point out to Wilbur that he wasn't a woman? I looked over to Josie. Stock-still, Josie posed, cheeks sucked in like an anorexic model and lips doing strange things. I groaned, "Wilbur, for God's sake—"

Wilbur threw up his hands and said, "Oh, all right. Josie, relax. Mr. B. is such a killjoy." Josie released her pose and grinned at both of us.

Wilbur fluttered his hands in front of himself. "Get Mr. Brown a Rice Krispie treat. Sweeten up that sour man," he said. Josephine obeyed and raced to the kitchen. Wilbur flung his hands to heaven again. Then the proud papa turned to me and said, "She made them herself."

Josephine stopped abruptly and darted a guilty glance back at Wilbur, who had put on his stricken face—her small mistake had become a mortal sin. Josie picked up the gooey snack off the counter and walked slow as molasses back to where I sat. Holding out the tray of treats, she repeated what Wilbur had already told me: "I made 'em myself." She added, "Daddy Wilbur doesn't want me to run 'cause he thinks I'll fall and go to the hospital again, but I know how to run without falling."

I propped Josie up on my lap. "It pays to be careful, sugar. Your daddy is concerned about you, that's all." I took the offered treat and nibbled like a rabbit around its edges. "Mmmm . . . good," I lied.

The doorbell downstairs rang and, like hounds, we each lifted our heads. Six rings sounded—the signal for apartment number six—Wilbur's apartment. Wilbur frowned.

"You expecting anybody?" I said.

Wilbur shook his head. Just then, Winnie bumped through Wilbur's door, carrying mounds of comfort and joy heaped high on a tray. I slid Josie off my lap, and stood to take the tray from her. Wilbur crossed over to the window that faced the street, raised it, and looked down below to the front steps.

"Oh my God, it's her," Wilbur said, pulling his head back in from the window. "She's at the front door."

"Who you talking about, Wilbur? Another guest? Shoot, the more the merrier is what I say." Winnie cruised to the window and looked over Wilbur's shoulder and peeked out. When she gasped aloud I knew something was up. She whispered in a too-loud voice, "Nothing to do but to let her in—for the child's sake."

All eyes fixed on Josie, and I clued in to what was going on and so did Josie.

"It's Mommy. It's Mommy," Josie screamed. She ran to the door, tugging on the handle to open it.

"No," shouted Wilbur harshly.

A well of tears in her eyes, Josie turned back. "But Daddy Wilbur, Mommy's come back like you said she would." Wilbur faltered, his eyes darting looks at Winnie and me and then back to Josie. Then he sucked air and belted his chartreuse smoking jacket so tightly around his middle I thought he would pop.

He said, "I told you not to run, Josie. Walk. Walk down the stairs." He paused and finally said. "And let your mother in."

Josie tipped out of the room in slow motion and headed down the stairs. We followed her out the door and stood in the hallway and watched as she descended. Of course, she picked up speed on the second landing and from there on out it was full speed ahead to the door.

In the entry hallway Josie disappeared from view, but we heard muffled voices raised in greeting and assumed an embrace between the two. Patty's loud sobbing drifted up the stairwell. Embarrassed, the three of us fidgeted for a moment before turning back into Wilbur's apartment. Once inside, we sat and waited for mother and daughter to return, each of us suddenly imprisoned in a cubicle of silence. I twiddled my thumbs, Winnie coughed, and Wilbur sat rooted like a vegetable. Seemed like I should leave, but Wilbur might think I was deserting him.

Two pairs of feet clumped heavily up the uncarpeted stairs, and then we heard fumbling outside the apartment door. Then Patty and Josie entered the apartment and my eyes popped open wider than Mt. Vesuvius exploding. Patty had matured. All evidence of the teenage Patty had disappeared. Hanging off her coat-hanger frame, Patty was decked out in a blue sable mink coat that dusted the floor. She looked as if she were a fashion model. One that needed to be fed some biscuits and a bowl of grits, quick.

Josephine hung from Patty's hand as if it would hurt to let go. Patty stayed glued to her child, the edges of pain stenciled on her face, and petted Josephine and stroked her cheeks.

Hard for Wilbur to witness this love between mother and child, so blatant and undiminished. He looked away. No two pairs of eyes met. I finally coughed and offered up a stupid comment, "Well, Patty, long time, no see."

Patty swiped away tears. "Uh, how you doing, Mr. Brown? Yeah, been a while. Good to see y'all." She glanced at Wilbur and said quickly, "Don't worry, I ain't staying long. Just long enough to give my baby her Christmas present."

Silence, then Wilbur cleared his throat and said, "Nobody's rushing you. About to serve dessert. Stay. For Josie's sake."

Patty glanced at her child. "Sure, sure," she said. Tired of all the foolishness, Winnie harrumphed and engulfed Patty in her large arms and bosomed chest. Patty woofed as the air was knocked out of her, but acquiesced to the enthusiastic embrace.

"Oh, sit down, girl," Winnie said, "and let me take your coat." She helped Patty wiggle out of the coat and added, "Child, is this for-real fur? Oowee, it's heavy. You must be doing all right." Winnie stroked the coat as if it were a pet.

"Must be doing better than all right," I said. "What you up to these days, Patty?"

As Winnie moved to hang the coat in Wilbur's closet, I kept my eyes focused on Patty. Her bright eyes avoided my gaze and her skittering movements gave her away.

"Oh, this and that," she replied.

Josie dragged her mother over to the couch. "Sit by me, Mommy, sit by me," she said.

"Sure, baby, Mommy'll sit by you."

Wilbur hustled to clear decorations off the couch and the two sat. Patty said, "About the other day, Wilbur—sorry—don't know what got into me—"

Wilbur shot a look in Josephine's direction and said, "Save it. Let's enjoy Christmas Eve."

Patty understood. She nodded and reached into her handbag and produced a tiny box wrapped in tinseled green and silver paper, topped with a dainty bow. To Josie she said, "For you."

Joy burst like fireworks from every pore of Josie's being. She bounced up and down on the couch like she had a spring in her butt. Then she turned to Wilbur and pleaded, "Daddy Wilbur, can I open it now? Please?"

"Sure, honey," he said. "One present before Christmas can't hurt. Right, Mr. B.?"

I jumped. Why the hell was he asking me? "Why not?" I said.

Josephine bounced some more and tore into the package like a hungry monster.

"Oooooooowee," she exclaimed, after opening it.

Wilbur leaned in to take a peek. "What is it?"

Josephine pulled a silver bracelet from the box and lifted it high for all to see. The letters of her name twirled off a silver chain and jangled in the quiet of the moment.

"Here, let me put it on you," said Patty.

Silently, we watched as Patty slid the tiny bracelet around Josephine's wrist and affixed the latch. Josephine wiggled her hand back and forth and a tinkling melody played. Then, in studied wonderment, she flipped each letter, one at a time, through her fingers. Finally she crushed her face into her mother's neck and mumbled a "Thank you, Mommy."

Patty hugged Josephine tightly and Wilbur got up to fix eggnog.

For the next hour we sat and chatted. The way civilized people supposedly do. Talking nothing and everything—you know how that goes. Everybody avoided the topic that sat like a pregnant buffalo in the middle of the room and that was all to the good.

Around nine, unable to keep her eyes open, Josie fell dead asleep, head laid across her mother's lap. Wilbur retrieved her, lifting her with some difficulty—and trundled the small bundle off to bed.

Couldn't help but see that the evening had taken its toll on him, strain evident on his face. Large onyx moons appeared beneath his eyes and his makeup had faded. Against the backdrop of blinking Christmas lights, lesions showed up, like tribal scars, across his cheeks and forehead.

Winnie slapped her knees, rose heavily, and called to Wilbur, "Honey child, I'm whipped and creamed. On my feet all day. Gonna do the same thing as Josie, put my butt and these feet of mine in bed." She rose. "See you tomorrow for dinner. My place. 'Night, all."

With Winnie's exit, two heavy sighs blew like baby tornadoes across the measures of space between Patty and myself. Then she, too, got up to leave. As she hefted her coat off a hanger from the closet, I said, "Still using, aren't you?"

Caught, she blinked and said, "I'm trying to quit."

"Question is, you succeeding?"

Patty hid her face in the folds of her fur—a way to avoid. "Got to get back to work."

"Tricking?"

A torch lit behind her eyes. "What's it to you, Mr. Brown? At least my bills get paid." Purse in hand, she marched to the door.

"Where'd you get the coat, Patty?"

"You need to mind your own damn business. I earned this coat. I make a good living."

"How do you do that? You'd better bottle the formula. Isn't it hard—with a drug habit?"

She spun around, eyes burning into me. Then she turned and slammed out the door. With the momentum of a fast and vicious memory, her heels receded down the winding stairwell. The finality of a death knell sounded as the front door swung shut behind her.

I stuffed my hands in my pockets, my mind racing. Patty's fur? I'd bet a dollar to a dime it came straight from the stolen Steadwell Collection.

Silent Night and Holy Shit.

Chapter 12

Christmas Day the house bustled with activity, the afternoon feast only hours away. My nostrils flanged with the odor of Christmas and I sniffed like I was doing a line of coke. Above me the floor creaked. I shuffled through my apartment, sipping frequently from a bottle of expensive brandy that Miss Ellie had dropped off. She shouldn't have. And on her social security check, too. I tipped back my head and swallowed.

Catherine's present sat propped up on a chair in the corner of my living room, bright and fussy and begging for attention. It stood out in the bleak atmosphere of my apartment with its shabby sofa, two black chairs, and piss-colored walls. For maybe the hundredth time since last year, I thought, *maybe it's time to fix this place up.*

It had been temporary digs since I moved in four years ago, and if you'd have asked me then, I never could have imagined it'd be my permanent nesting place. Thoughts of my old Sugar Hill residence and yesteryear jetted through my mind, but those days were gone and naw, I didn't miss the life.

I looked around again. But damn, this place was depressing. Ought to at least throw a holly or two around to spruce it up.

My Aunt Reba, who raised me—sort of—until I went off to jail, didn't believe in Christmas. A lapsed Seventh Day Adventist became her excuse for not honoring the festive celebration of the holiday—nor did she give presents.

Her death last year brought not a single tear to my eye. Because of life with Reba it took hard work each year to shift from morose to okay during the holidays. The brandy helped. Dropping off presents early this morning like I was a Harlem Santa Claus helped, too. Pockets were empty but my heart was full.

Scattered on the floor were presents and cards from tenants. Times were tough, so each gift meant something beyond the gift. A tin of baked cookies, a cheap bottle of aftershave, homemade hogshead cheese, five pairs of socks, and oh yes, brandy. Which reminded me.

I sipped some more and the phone rang. I shouted into the receiver my best Kris Kringle imitation, "Merry Christmas." The brandy made me do it. A gruff West Indian voiced barked in my ear, "What you say, Merry, eh? Funning an old lady, is you now, Amos?"

Catherine's mother. Used to have good times with her, but I hadn't heard from her after me and Catherine called it quits. Her call was unexpected. "Mrs. Walters? Sorry about the loss of your brother . . ."

"Sorry? Now you *is* funning me. Harry was a son of a bitch and you know it."

Okay, he was. But I didn't think she'd say so.

"You got plans?" she said.

"For today? The tenants and I are having Christmas dinner together."

"Too bad. You could have had Christmas dinner with us." I didn't respond to that and waited while Mrs. Walters hacked up phlegm. She came back on the line and said, "Well then, come by Saturday, after me brother Harry planted in the ground, need to talk with you."

I recognized an order when I heard it, so I agreed.

"Bring change," she said. "We can play Tonk."

"No more canasta?"

"Canasta make me butt tired."

"What do you need to talk about?"

"Find out Saturday. Catherine don't know."

Clickup and she was gone. Well, no need trying to figure out what Mrs. Walters wanted—Saturday would be soon enough.

I strolled over to the stereo and turned it on. I chose LPs of R&B Christmas carols and bumped up the volume. Then I hunched myself into the tired black chair and clawed at the stubble on my chin. A bluesy "Merry Christmas, Baby" bounced off the walls, and me and Charles Brown serenaded everybody within earshot. I danced around the room, bumping and grinding in my undershorts, and otherwise making a fool of myself. Felt good. Outside, snow melted under a bright sun; the weather contrary, it portended a sunny Christmas Day. Fuck a duck. No snow? I sipped more brandy and wiggled my backside deeper into my chair while Smokey Robinson and the Miracles blared out a version of "God Rest Ye Merry Gentlemen." What? I leaned forward to listen. All vanilla-flavored music with a chocolate twist? Well, all right. I leaned back, scratched my balls, and then the phone rang.

"This Tishonda," she said.

"Tishonda who?" I hooted, like some owl.

"This Amos Brown I'm talking to, ain't it? Come quick. Steadwell's back in his apartment, screaming his head off again and acting crazy."

I sat up. Oh, *that* Tishonda.

I told her okay, I'd be there, and slammed down the phone. I threw on some clothes and then, of course, spent the next ten minutes searching for my goddam keys—why the hell did I always misplace my keys? It was a curse. I gulped more brandy. I had an epiphany and then I remembered where I had left my keys. I scurried to the kitchen, snatched them off the sink, and headed out the door. Shit. Wasted ten minutes. Steadwell might have taken off.

I flew to my car and scrambled in. First time I'd been in Sugar since last week's storm. The car had been neglected, winter filth covered its hood. I hadn't a garage to store her in, one of the disadvantages of living life in the city.

Shit. I squinted. Crud coated the glass on Sugar's front windows. I could barely see two feet in front of me. I grabbed a scraper out of the glove compartment, jumped back out of the car, and scraped the last of the snow off of the windows, grateful for the sun and the meltdown. but knowing I had lost another five minutes.

Then I eased back into the car, bumping my butt across Sugar's leather seat. Damn. The leather felt old and stiff and needed re-conditioning. Like a guilty husband, I patted the dashboard and promised Sugar I'd make it up to her. I switched the engine on and the car immediately purred. Good old Sugar, good old antifreeze. *Jingle bells, jingle bells, jingle all the wa-a-y* . . . I sang as I pulled away from the curb.

The drive through Harlem was not without Christmas Day peril—skates, bikes, and trikes banged into each other, and pint-sized critters swarmed the sidewalks and playgrounds. The streets were jumping and the activity must have discouraged the crack-heads and the hopheads. They'd slithered back into their holes and were nowhere to be seen—the turf given over to the kids today. I made it to Steadwell's in record time.

Chapter 13

Made no difference—I was too late. Steadwell's apartment had been ransacked. Drawers hung open, a table had been tipped and Steadwell nowhere in sight. Tishonda beat her breast, but what was the point? Not her fault. Even if she'd called the cops instead of me, they wouldn't have made it here any sooner. In this neck of the woods the cops were known for their slow response. And on Christmas Day, too?

I asked Tishonda, "You said you heard Steadwell screaming—was he yelling at somebody, do you think?"

"I don't know. He was just yelling—same way he did before. Not sure if he was yelling at someone—and I was too scared to barge in."

"I understand. You heard him leave?"

"Noise, then quiet—that's what I heard. Didn't hear anyone come in or out. You arrived and that's it."

A breeze drifted past my neck. The apartment was chilly. I glanced around. A window had been left open, and I crossed over to it and poked my head out, leaning over the edge—the window opened on to a fire escape. Even with the disappearing snow, traces of man-made tracks led away from the window and down to the alley below.

I stilled my breathing for a moment, listening. The alley was silent as a cemetery—not a creature stirred, not even a louse. I drew my head back in and reflected. Somebody had exited down the fire escape. Was Steadwell up to that? At his age?

For the first time I felt a glimmer of dread. Whoever the intruder had been, it was obvious he had been searching for something. What the hell was he looking for? He had passed up Steadwell's merchandise stacked in boxes around the room. Shit, where the fuck was Steadwell? Not dead, I hoped.

The front door still hung wide open. I picked my way back through the clutter and shut it, keeping myself alert to any clue that might tell me what had happened.

Confounding me was the fact that Steadwell's inventory had been left untouched. Stacked high in one corner were boxes of unopened stereos. Along another wall were row upon row of boxes of bathroom fixtures, and on top of those were sealed boxes of a product called Mr. Handy-Dandy's Handy Tools. Hmm. What the hell, I opened a box. Wrenches, screwdrivers, the usual assortment. I deliberated and set one aside—I figured Steadwell owed me—then just as quickly got back to business, guiltily reminding myself that he was missing.

It hit me that this stuff must be a recent haul or the cops would have confiscated it when they arrested Steadwell. Perspiration glistened on my knuckles. I shook my head in amazement. Steadwell boosting while out on bail? The man had more nerve than Superman.

What if the cops had discovered this shit? Good thing Tishonda hadn't called them. They'd have buried Steadwell's ass.

I glanced over at Tishonda, who fidgeted nervously, eyes darting everywhere. "You live alone?" I said. "Before I call the police, we need to move this stuff."

A college girl, she understood immediately.

"You can store it in my place," she said. "It's only me left in the apartment. My mom died last April."

She said it matter-of-factly and turned away from my stare. Then she picked up a Handy-Dandy box and hefted it on her shoulder. I followed suit. For over an hour, we carted the stolen merchandise across the hall to her apartment. When we finished, I called the cops.

And then we waited. And waited some more. Two hours drifted by like a lazy summer afternoon. Aromas of cooking food coming out of nearby apartments assailed my nose. Made me crazy. The smells flowed like gravy under Steadwell's door and wheedled through the pores of the walls. Umph. Poor or not, the fact is, black folks cook on holidays and that's the natural truth. Nobody did it better and nobody deserved a meal more. I theorized it to be a form of entitlement left over from slavery days. It was a Negro thing, back in the day when we used to call ourselves Negroes.

Tishonda sat at the kitchen table, rocking in her chair, her arms wrapped across her belly. She smelled it too—probably hungry the same as me. In my head, chains of string beans catapulted over crusty brown turkeys. The vision expanded to dizzying images of candied yams, mashed potatoes, baked ham with cloves and pine-apple and my belly started bawling. I stood up and almost keeled over, so delirious was I from hunger.

I crossed to the window to get a breath of fresh air and that's when I noticed the bullet hole, pristine and perfect, in the center of the window. I didn't see blood, but the bullet hole unnerved me.

I steadied myself. Fuck the cops. I decided to lock up the place and get out of there. I let Tishonda know we were leaving and searched Steadwell's belongings for his apartment keys. In case I had to get back in. Did he keep a spare? I considered myself a bona fide expert at finding keys. Didn't I spend most of my waking days looking for mine? As it turned out, it didn't take much effort to lo-cate Steadwell's spare keys. I found them hidden, of all places, under his doormat. Arrogant motherfucker. As if the old man dared anyone to burgle his crib. Just goes to show you.

I locked up and noticed the forlorn look on Tishonda's face. The kid was alone. It was Christmas, and if anybody knew how that felt, I did. So what did I do? Hell, I invited her to my brownstone to join the tenants for Christmas dinner. Under Winnie's wing, she'd do fine. No sense in both of us missing a meal.

After I dropped her off, I gunned the motor and headed Sugar over to the 28th Precinct. One thing, I didn't like to be ignored, even by cops. If a call wouldn't bring them, to get in their faces was the next best thing. I intended to raise hell or the dead, whichever came first.

Chapter 14

So what happened when I got there? The precinct's desk sergeant chewed on a wad of gum and ignored me big-time, even with me standing in front of him, staring at his pork chop face. I could have been talking to the moon. He remained steadfast and silent while I jabbered and explained. Was he mentally deficient? Not my fault he had the holiday shift.

With each wasted minute, I got a little more crazy. Steadwell was missing, maybe murdered. I got belligerent and started shouting. When that didn't move him, I brought out the big guns. I named every person I knew who might have juice—and believe me, I could name a few. You work the other side of the law long enough, you know how that works.

I threw out Bill Bundt's name and finally got his attention, his face lighting up like a pinball machine.

"*Captain* Bundt? Why didn't you say so? What'd you say your name was?"

I licked my lips and stifled a response. For the fifth time, I told him my name. This time he seemed to get it. He picked up the phone and repeated my name into it, then turned back to me, pleased, like he'd done something special.

"Captain Bundt says go up. Third floor." He dismissed me with a flick of his thumb.

My face warm, I ascended the stairs and wondered if the meeting with Bundt would go any better. Last time I'd seen Bundt he hadn't been too happy with me. Of course, he got credit for that major collar I dumped in his lap four years ago—it probably earned him his promotion. But would he remember that? Probably not. Knowing Bundt, he'd focus on the negatives. Like all the trouble I caused him while I was doing it.

When I reached the third floor, Bundt stood in the doorway, ready to greet me. Well, maybe *greet* was the wrong word.

"Is it Amos Brown, the fucking mortician? Find another fucking body, Amos—is that why you're fucking here?"

I let his invectives roll over me. "Chill, man," I said, and put my hands in my pockets. Funny, four years ago his vocabulary hadn't been so limited. His eyes curdled as he glared at me. No, the man wasn't happy to see me.

"Bundt. A surprise to find you here. Why aren't you at home with your family?" I said.

Boom. A seismic rumbling rippled through Bundt like a loud and treacherous fart; his face turned beet-red. "Fucking asshole, fucking wiseguy, eh? What, you think I don't have one?" Spittle flew from his mouth. "Business brought me in. Which I should be taking care of instead of talking to you. Whaddaya want, Brown?"

Umph. The man was in the middle of a divorce, no doubt about it. Bundt's jowls quivered as he spoke; I watched them flap. He had put on a lot of weight, too. I got quickly to why I was there, "A friend's missing. Your sergeant downstairs gave me some song and dance about Father Time. Way I see things, there's no time to waste. Been to my friend's apartment—it's trashed. Definitely evidence of foul play. It's something for the cops, that's why I'm here."

Bundt drew his eyebrows together. "More," he said. I briefed him about the circumstances of Steadwell's disappearance, leaving out the incriminating stuff. Somewhere in the discussion I mentioned Steadwell was out on bail on a murder charge.

Bundt's expression changed and he unknit his eyebrows. "Foul play, my ass. You're tied in a sling 'cause your friend has skipped, leaving you holding the bag. The bail bag. Sounds like you're going to be out bail money. That's what it sounds like."

Until that moment I hadn't even thought of the bail. But now that he mentioned it . . . My stomach floated to my feet like the ball dropping in Times Square on New Year's Eve. No, it hadn't crossed my mind. But now I realized personal jeopardy and everything I owned was attached to Steadwell's disappearance. Today was Saturday. Steadwell had to show up in court on Tuesday.

I ran my tongue past my teeth and said, "I called the cops to a scene of a break-in four hours ago. Nobody showed up—that's why I'm here in person to file a report. This is an old man we're talking about—he might have been taken hostage. He might be dead." I paused. "I think you owe me, *Captain* Bundt."

I didn't blatantly suggest that I was responsible for his promotion, but his neck colored pink, so I thought the possibility existed. The color began in his neck and quickly moved to his head like mercury rising in a thermometer. He made a choking sound and I thought one of his blood vessels might rupture.

"Easy, Bundt, easy," I said.

His voice shook. "Get this, Brown. I was happy being a lieutenant. My family was happy. Now all I get is stress and duress. All because of you." And then he jerked a thumb in the direction of a young cop sitting nearby at a desk. I looked to where he pointed and Bundt stuttered, unable to get the words out fast enough, "Sharpe, take this man's f-fucking statement." Then he gave me the evil eye and strode off.

A half-hour later I was still sitting with the young cop, who typed with the speed of a two-fingered turtle. Sharpe's last typo had him churning the copies of the report around and around in the typewriter's roller—unable to pry them loose. No kidding, the man should've been named anything but Sharpe. I was getting impatient, more time wasted. The phone rang and Sharpe picked it up.

"Officer Sharpe. May I help you?" Then he paused. "Yessir." He listened a moment longer, then whipped his head toward Captain Bundt's empty office. "He's not in. Can I take a message, sir?"

Face bunched in a knot, he scribbled a note on a pad while I scratched the stubble on my face. Jesus, been here long enough to grow a beard. Suddenly Sharpe straightened in his chair. He shouted yes, yes, yes, and trembled like he was going to come. I leaned away. Then he slammed down the receiver and scrawled furiously, filling the pad and mumbling, "Jewel-heist-investigation-moving-uptown. Hot damn. Wait 'til Captain Bundt hears this. Wow." Then he upturned an excited face to me and confided, "Know who that was? The commissioner himself. Uh, how do you spell commissioner? With two m's?"

"Two m's, two s's. Look, can we get back to me?"

"Got to give the captain this message."

And then the sucker dashed off. No I'm sorry, no excuse me, no nothing. Minutes ticked by. Cops drifted in and out of the room and shot curious glances at me. I stewed in my juices until I couldn't take it anymore. After a half-hour, I knew I had been forgotten. I put my hat on my head and left the building.

Fuck a donkey, I'll find Steadwell my damn self.

The events at the precinct made me kick cans in front of me all the way back to my car. I thought, a jewel robbery, the police get all excited. Let some brother's life be in danger—that don't count for nothing. Big Kahunas working the case, who gives a flying crap? Uptown action, my ass. Cops know good and well ain't no nigger in Harlem have the juice to pull off a stunt like that. Brother'd have to have downtown connections for that.

Well, maybe somebody like Harry the Monkey Chaser could have caused the deed to be done, but Harry was dead. Oh hell, it didn't take a genius. I knew what that was about. Can't solve the crime, blame it on some dumb niggers. Don't matter who. Anybody with a rap sheet and a criminal record. Satisfy the mayor, police commissioner, insurance companies, everybody. Pick up some Harlem thief that's innocent and blame the crime on him. After all, what can some dumb nigger do? Complain?

I caught myself. Innocent thief. How nuts was that? In spite of myself, I smiled. An oxymoron, that's what that was. I chuckled some more and crunched snow beneath my feet as I made my way to my car. But somewhere in the middle of the street my legs stopped working, slowed down, and I suddenly froze. Comprehension started in my thighs and raced to my cranium. Holy shit.

Day broke inside my brain and walloped me mightily upside the head and made my mouth fly open. *Awww, shit, no.*

Two cops standing fifty feet from the precinct door eyed me suspiciously. In front of me was another can. I kicked it hard. It turned out to be a rock, covered with snow. Pain shot to the top of my head and zinged back down to my foot. Oh, my Gawwwd . . .

The two cops eased over toward me, hands poised above their holsters.

I shouted, "Merry Christmas," and scrambled to my car, and left them standing bewildered. Had to find Steadwell. Best to hit the streets. In Harlem Village news spread fast. Somebody had to know something. I found the nearest pay phone and dropped a dime in the slot. Would Steadwell have tried to call me? I let the phone ring for a long time. When there was no pickup, I grimaced and hung up. Didn't turn on my machine.

Time. Time was my enemy. Steadwell had been missing for four hours. I glanced at my watch. Make that five.

Me and Sugar cruised to a few spots in the 'hood and I checked inside. The Lenox Lounge, the Red Rooster. Nothing. I swung by another club off of 145th Street, known to be a favorite Steadwell hangout. Zip.

Stalled in traffic off Eighth Avenue, I wondered what place to hit next. I peered through Sugar's windows and noticed I was not far from Poontang Wanda's. Though it had been a while since I had seen her, I decided that if anybody would know something, it would be Wanda. I swung out of traffic, apologized to Sugar, bounced over curb and sidewalk, and headed over to Wanda's.

A stretch limousine was parked out in front of her place and on the driver's side, a curl of smoke wafted up and out of a crack in the window. Wanda had settled into one of the few chic enclaves left in Harlem, three streets north of Strivers Row. Like I remembered when I was a kid growing up in Harlem, Christmas wreaths hung merrily on most of the brownstones' doors. Still, I locked my car up tight—couldn't be too careful—and ascended the steps to Wanda's establishment. The limo driver kept his eyes on me and I kept mine on him, both of us suffering from the distrust and paranoia of our times.

It took a few minutes before the maid, dressed in a frilly outfit that looked as if she'd jumped off the screen of some English flick, finally opened the door.

"You have an appointment, sir?" she said with a slight lisp.

"Tell Wanda, Amos Brown is here."

"Sorry, Ms. Plessant doesn't see clients anymore."

My eyes bucked. I hoped to God not. Wanda was in her seventies. "Not a client—this is personal business. Amos Brown. She'll see me."

The maid clucked her tongue in disapproval and didn't move, but I wasn't intimidated. If she got tough I could take her. All five feet, 115 pounds of her. Then her frown made me understand that she wasn't programmed to make decisions, hence her immobility. "Just tell Wanda I'm here. It's okay, really. I'll wait here, right inside the door."

That mollified her. She let me into the foyer. I leaned against a wall and checked out her legs as she strutted away from me. When she looked back, I hadn't moved, so she continued walking, her heels clicking sharp across the polished hardwood floors that led to Wanda's inner sanctum nestled deep inside the bowels of the house.

Fifteen long minutes it took. So I copped a seat in the sitting room, taking advantage of the purpose of the room, until at last the maid's shoes clicked down the hallway again. Heels tippy-tapped past the sitting room on the way to the foyer. When the heels stopped I sensed the maid's confusion, so I stood in the doorway and called, "Yoo-hoo."

I didn't expect the reaction. She jumped out of her socks, or nylons, or whatever it was she had on her legs, and accused immediately, "You said you'd stand in the foyer."

I shrugged. "You were gone a long time. My feet hurt."

"Ms. Plessant was at dinner. She's finished and she'll see you now," she said, a snake hissing behind her tongue. For someone with a lisp, to have an employer named Plessant had to be a personal challenge.

My stomach barked like a Chihuahua—I couldn't help it. The maid heard it and jumped again and then rolled her eyes at me.

Poontang Wanda was a handsome woman who had broad features and a broader ass. Yet, in her seventies, she still had an awe-inspiring figure—one of those hourglass-shaped ones, and except for the fact that her caboose had gotten a little loose and drooped a little in the back, Wanda had held it together. Now she turned back with a drink in her hand, a fine blend of Scotch whiskey, and passed it across to me. Yep, Wanda was class. I sipped and nodded my appreciation.

"Must be trouble, huh, Amos? Why else you here?"

No pussyfooting with Wanda—I liked that about her. "Right, Wanda. You know Deacon Steadwell?"

She frowned. "Sure, I know him—longtime. We've done plenty of business together."

"He's missing. I hope he isn't dead."

She put her drink down and sat in her Queen Anne chair, perched ramrod-straight, like royalty herself, and said quietly, "What's happened?"

"Hoping you could tell me. Steadwell's been charged with Dap Jones's murder—"

"Yeah, I heard."

"Supposed to have killed Dap over some stolen fur coats. Steadwell said he didn't do it. He's out on bail, but he's been throwing around revenge threats. Somebody might have taken him seriously."

"He's missing? And you think I may have heard where he is?"

"You hear a lot, Wanda. Steadwell's gone missing in the last couple of hours. Nobody popped him in his apartment—I figure they're holding him."

"Who and why?"

I shrugged my shoulders. "That's what I need to find out. You got any ideas?"

"Give me a minute." She sipped her Scotch. I waited.

When she put her drink down, she asked, "Where's the coats? Find the coats, bet you'll find Steadwell."

I blinked. Could the old coot have the missing coats? But someone trashed his apartment. Why? They couldn't have been looking for the coats. Eighteen fur coats you can't miss—you don't need to trash an apartment to find them. But what Wanda said made sense. I wondered again about Patty. And wondered if there were any more coats floating around Harlem.

"Any of your girls shown up in fur lately?"

Wanda snorted. "Fur what? Look, I'm barely making it. If I ain't making it, you know my girls ain't making it, either. Where are they going to get a fur coat? We're in a tough economy. Shoot, if it weren't for my investments, I'd have been out of business a long time ago.

"I'm waiting it out, business has to turn around, but these drug addicts are killing me. Competition is fierce. How can my girls compete with them? Sure, a few people'll pay top dollar for class, but they won't come to Harlem anymore to get it. The druggies are scaring them away. That's why I have a take-out service now."

"Food?"

"No, fool. Pussy. The doctors, lawyers, and Indian Chiefs call me—I send my girls out to service them. Got a car and driver to accommodate to-the-door service."

That explained the limo. "That is classy, Wanda."

"You got that right. But it's costing me. Some of my girls have gotten sick, too."

I raised an eyebrow.

"Your girls get their shots, don't they?"

"Of course, don't be foolish. Remmie? Remember her? Got terrible sick. And it ain't claps, or syphilis, or nothing like that. I swear, I don't know what's going around. The poor child couldn't even stand on her own power when she left. I gave her some money and she went back down south to her momma.

Sweetie-pie's another one—still in the hospital and she ain't getting no better. I've been cracking down on the girls—reminding them to use condoms. It's something else, Amos. Something else is out there that the government's not telling us about."

I have to admit, Wanda looked worried. She sighed. "I should have opened a mom-and-pop store. Better for my constitution and my pocketbook."

"Wouldn't have worked, Wanda."

"Why not?"

"You need a Pop for that."

"I got your Pop, hanging. That ain't never stopped me."

Wanda liked girls better than men, and she was known to have a girlfriend or two on the side. I smiled and Wanda returned my smile and said, "Well, let that be a lesson to you—better not do anything stupid."

Up went my eyebrow again.

"Sex-wise," Wanda said, and leaned forward.

"I've been a monk, Wanda."

"Yeah, well, hope your monk wears a hood."

I shifted in my seat. "Jesus, Wanda—how'd we get to talking about my sex life?" I laughed nervously. "Woman, my sex life ain't none of your business."

"Didn't say that twenty years ago."

I colored and wriggled some more in my chair. It was Wanda's turn to laugh and she hooted.

"Just out of prison, didn't know what to do with that worm."

"Wanda, please."

"I showed you what to do with it, didn't I?"

"Wanda—"

"Well, didn't I?"

I looked at her, my face hot and embarrassed. All those years ago, it was Poontang Wanda saw to it that I was educated in the ways of the world. A social cripple, I spent my teenage years behind bars.

Since I was big and burly, no one ever bothered me inside the joint, but I'd never been schooled in social graces and certainly had never dated. That part of my life never happened. It was true—I hadn't known what to do with my 'worm,' but Wanda did. And here she was, making fun.

She threw back her head and chortled again. "Okay, okay, let's talk about something else. Another drink? What about Steadwell's old girlfriend? You talked to her?"

I looked down at my glass. The scotch had disappeared. "Hit me up a skosh, Wanda—and what girlfriend you talking about?" She poured a short shot into my glass.

"The one with the red hair."

"He stopped going with her twenty years ago."

"So you say. Hmph, he didn't stop doing her."

My mouth gaped open and Wanda launched into another topic.

"Prince is handling Steadwell's case, is that right, Amos? How's he doing—haven't heard from him in a long while."

"Uh, he's okay," I said. "Planning to go into politics."

"Figured he'd do something like that. Perhaps that's why he's keeping his distance." She paused. "Until he wants something."

"With all the politicians you do business with? Hasn't stopped them—"

"Yeah, well, nobody said Prince was smart. Intelligent, yes, but not smart like you, Amos."

I nodded. I knew what she meant. "Let's hope he's intelligent enough to do something for Steadwell. Look here, I'd better get going—" I stood and Wanda did the same.

"Sure. If I hear anything, Amos, I'll let you know."

The door cracked open and a head popped in, followed by a chest and two magnificent titties. "Hazel? Is that you?" Wanda said. "Come in. Let me introduce you to an old friend."

No two ways about it, her titties were a wonder, and I gawked. I was extremely impressed with the top half of Hazel and when the rest of her tall and willowy body made it through the door in a slinky silver blue evening gown, I gasped—and it wasn't just because of her looks. Slung carelessly over one arm was a floor-length sable mink.

She got Wanda too. Wanda choked on her drink and blurted, "Where the hell did you get that fur?"

Where indeed?

Chapter 15

Wanda repeated, "Hazel, answer me—where did you get that fur?"

Hazel stroked the fur and said, "Hot stuff, isn't it?"

"Mind if I look at the label?" I said, and crossed over to her. Hazel panicked and held tightly to her coat. Bit by bit I had to pry it out of her arms. Understandably, she didn't want to let go.

Wanda barked sharply, "Hazel, let the man see the label."

I checked the label and my eyes met Wanda's. "Katz Furs. Hazel, baby, you have no idea how hot. Boyfriend? Or did you purchase this yourself?"

"Shoots, me? Nuh-uh, ain't making that kind of money. A gentleman friend gave it to me yesterday—a Christmas present, he said."

Wanda said, "Someone you met here?"

Hazel shot Wanda a frightened look. "No, he's just a guy I been—uh, dating."

"Dating? Where'd he say he got it from?"

Hazel's eyes darted nervously back and forth between me and Wanda, her answer a *Jeopardy* response, more question than answer. "The . . . store?" she said.

"Where could I find this boyfriend of yours?" I asked. Tears bubbled from Hazel's eyes.

"You're not going to hurt him, are you?"

I reassured her, "I just want to talk to him, that's all. Don't get upset. Your boyfriend might help me locate a missing friend."

Wanda confirmed this with a nod of her head.

Hazel said, "He's got a wife or something, so I always meet him at the Fletcher Arms. He lives up in Dobbs Ferry, I think. I've seen train tickets from there in his wallet."

Wanda scowled and took a step forward. "You going through his wallet? I've taught you better than that."

I interceded before Wanda popped her one. "Got a name?" I said.

She darted looks back at Wanda. "Ralphie. Uh, Ralph Evinrude."

"Like the motor?"

Hazel blanked on me.

"Never mind. Evinrude. When are you meeting Ralphie Evinrude next?"

Hazel shrugged her shoulders. "We meet at his apartment in town. Once a week, maybe twice a week, he calls me. He's with his family today."

"Next time he calls, let Wanda know. I need to speak to him."

Wanda patted the girl. "It's all right, Hazel. Nobody's mad at you. Sure, she'll let me know. Now get going to your next appointment, or you'll be late."

Hazel scurried out of the room, glad to be rid of the scrutiny. Two coats in two days—no coincidence. Katz Furs, huh? I needed to talk to Patty again and I had an idea where I'd find her.

"What're you thinking?" Wanda said.

I set my drink down. "What am I thinking? Here I am in the middle of a candy store and I'm leaving to chase down a chocolate drop."

"I'm not asking what that means." Wanda's eyes crinkled, I pecked her on the cheek and left.

Nighttime, and Patty would be working the streets—not exclusive goods, like Hazel, but the million-dollar question had to be, did every prostitute in Harlem have a fur coat?

Well, maybe eighteen of them did.

* * *

Gangs of kids scuttled through the streets like water beetles on speed. I rolled down the windows to hasten the defrosting process and their laughter rolled into my car like tumbleweed, voices innocent and carefree. It grieved me to know that half these boys would be jailed within the year.

I pulled up to a light, next to a group of preteens hanging on the corner. One kid loudly batted the dozens around with his friends, bragging about what he got for Christmas and signifying on those who didn't get anything. Insults flew like bullets. I'd guess the less a kid received for Christmas, the more he blustered and the more he cracked on his friends.

Shades of my own childhood. What doesn't kill you makes you stronger, ain't that what they say? Soporific for the underclass— keeping you always on the edge of hope. Add another callus to your spirit. I waved to the group and they waved back, and I eased through the light as it changed to green.

I passed hookers trolling on Seventh Avenue, shivering in scanty clothes worn to entice. Of course, the hooker I was looking for was cozy in a comfy fur coat. And where was she? I stopped a few girls and asked them if they knew Patty. They responded in the negative.

My watch said ten o'clock. I stopped by my house to switch on my answering machine—just in case. The brownstone quiet. Everyone probably in for the night. I went to some other hooker-hangouts but no luck. Finally, I decided to swing by the Flash Inn. More upscale clientele in that establishment. Patty's fur coat would get her through the door, and as I recalled, Dap occasionally hung out at the bar.

I headed over to Macombs Place where Harlem's gourmands gathered. My stomach rumbled and I was a little light-headed. Forget the sugarplums—the idea of prime rib danced in my head— and at the Flash Inn's bar, gossip flowed like a river.

I ordered dinner and then rubbed shoulders with the patrons at the oval bar. None of the regulars had seen Steadwell. Patty's name was unfamiliar. The subject of Dap Jones surfaced, and everybody offered an opinion. I listened.

"Say man, yeah, I heard about Dap. If Steadwell did him in, I say three cheers for Steadwell. Dap wasn't worth the paper it takes to wipe my ass."

From the other end of the bar someone responded, "Why you say that? That's cold, man. Dap never done nothing to you, did he?"

"I'm the only one he hasn't done something to."

Another voice, "Don't believe that nigger—reason Henry's jaw-juicing is because Dap did him in—stole one of his whores right out from under him—ask Sweets, he'll tell you."

"Why you put Sweets in it, nigger, if you talking to me?"

"I'm talking to you now 'cause you ain't got over it."

"You don't know nothing. For your information—Dap ain't stole no woman from me. Stole my money, that's what he stole. No-good Dap would've stolen Christ off the cross if he hadn't been nailed down."

Next to me, a bass voice cut through the laughter. Sweets Monroe's voice rumbled out of the depths of his portly frame, "That's the problem, ain't it? Dap always taking what don't belong to him. That's why people had it in for him."

Sweets played a mean jazz saxophone and found it unnecessary to float a lot of backwash out of his mouth, so when he talked, most folks listened. I was listening now.

"What people you talking about, Sweets?" I said as I ambled down the bar and copped myself a spot next to him.

Sweets lowered his voice. "Them Eye-talians, for one."

I raised an eyebrow. "The Mob? Dap was lightweight—he didn't have nothing to do with the Italians, did he?"

"He be trying."

I ordered a drink—Scotch, water back—and sat down on a stool next to Sweets, told the bartender to tighten up Sweets's drink. "Drugs?" I asked.

"Oh, Dap always into drugs—that's how he kept his women in line—but not big-time. Harry had the corner on that."

"You don't think he was muscling Harry?"

Sweets let go a raspberry. I nodded, said, "Guess not. No brains. So what else would the Mob want from him?"

"I plays my axe and minds my business, that's what I does." Sweets's eyes played over the room, cautious. "I'd advise you to do the same, Amos." Over in the dining area Uptown met Downtown, and customers came from far away as Queens and Long Island. I didn't blame Sweets for being careful. You never could tell who might be in the place scarfing down a dish of penne puttanesca or prime rib. Sweets downed his drink and raised his haunches one cheek at a time off the bar stool.

I touched his arm. "Got a name to share, Sweets?" Sweets looked unhappily at my hand resting on his arm and paused. Then he murmured so low I almost couldn't hear him, "Sergio—gots a droopy moustache, tiny eyes. He drops by Wells for chicken and waffles in the early A.M.—but you ain't heard it from me. Him and Dap was tight for a minute. Be cool. Watch your back, man."

It was Sweets's back that I watched as he exited the bar—his back the size of a Mack truck, no lie. From down the bar somebody shouted, "Hey, Amos, man, you born in Harlem?"

I looked at the man—where was this going?

"Harlem Hospital. I guess you'd call that Harlem."

"Sure you wasn't born in Louisiana? Or Mississippi? Maybe North Carolina? 'Cause ain't no nigger I ever heard of, named Amos, born in Harlem." He turned to the man next to him. "Is you? Is you ever hear of anybody else named Amos born in Harlem?"

Black folks don't need no television when they got themselves. Bump into any five Negroes on a corner or in a bar, and you're set for at least five hours of pure entertainment.

The entertainment portion of the program was starting now. The entire bar joined in riffing on my name. "What the hell your momma thinking?" someone else said. "Ain't nobody in Harlem name of Amos."

I kept sipping on my drink, taking it for a while, while they played the dozens. It wasn't like I hadn't heard it before. Then I said, "Somebody named Catastrophe going talk about *my* name?"

Indignant, the brother screamed. "What the hell you talking about? My name Cat. Named Cat 'cause I'm so slick."

"Huh, Nigger, you slick 'cause of that Murray's grease you slap on your head."

My people, my people. The topic of conversation was nicknames, and Little Koochie—named because he was a pussy—started sermonizing. I went to the pay phone and called myself to check for messages. Nothing. Koochie's teasing tenor voice drifted over.

"Yeah, baby, just show up at a nigger's funeral, that's how you find out they real name," he said. "Froggy? Remember him, with the big eyes? His real name, the one his momma give him—Clyde Tisdale, the third. Now what kind of name is that, y'all? At his funeral—everybody bust out soon's they heard his name—happiest funeral you ever did see. Niggers couldn't stop they laughing. His ex-wives laughed the loudest—first time they ever heard his real name."

The bar roared. I dialed Steadwell's number, hoping by some miracle he had returned to his place. A crazy idea. No one answered. When Victor the waiter told me my table was ready, I gladly left the hyenas at the bar and trotted to the dining room, I was that hungry.

Chapter 16

Last night I had a good meal and a lot to drink. Today it backed up on me. I belched and fire exploded through my nose. I needed to take a recess from this drinking. I didn't find Patty. I never found Steadwell. Sergio I forgot about. The after-tinsel effects of Christmas had caught up with me. I was in a stupor the morning after Christmas, my body bloated and heavy as I gazed with leaden awareness at early street activity through my office window.

I rubbed my face. I could use some sleep. My problems had compounded. Not only was I searching for Steadwell, I had added Patty, Ralphie, and now this Sergio guy to my list. Welcome to the Brown Detective Agency, seeker of lost persons. So far, 0 for 0. That wasn't too good, was it?

Better inform Prince what's up with Steadwell. I reached for the phone, all the while knowing that Prince and company probably wouldn't be at the office today, but still, I gave it a shot.

The phone rang a long time. Just as I was about to hang up, a questioning *hello* sounded through the wires—Prince, sounding as surprised as me.

"Prince. Bad news," I said. "Steadwell's disappeared."

A silence and then, "Shit. Shit."

"Somebody's holding him—or, he's dead."

"Give it to me, Amos. All of it."

I related what I had found at Steadwell's apartment and that I reported him missing.

Prince said, "Listen, I've filed motions, we're expected back in court December 30—next Tuesday. If Steadwell doesn't show up, say bye-bye to your bail."

"What if he's dead?"

"That would work."

"What?"

"Amos—cold facts, that'd be the only excuse. Pray that Steadwell hasn't flown the coop."

I hung up slowly. Less than five days. I sat in my desk chair and swiveled and then rocked. Josephine's gift of a candy cane rested in the middle of my desk on top of the *New York Times*. I picked up the red-striped candy and sucked. Cobwebs lifted from my brain.

I didn't bother to read the newspaper. I didn't want more bad news so I stuffed it in the wastebasket. But I noticed the banner headline. The jewel thief hadn't been caught—not yet—the headline said so.

I twirled in my swivel chair and sucked some more. If Steadwell's running, where would he go? The man never ventured out of New York City. No, that was wrong. Me and Steadwell used to make runs up to Sarasota to bet on the ponies. Would he go there? No, that made no sense. Steadwell was still in Harlem. I'd bet on it.

Did the old man ransack his own place to throw me off the scent? The footprints left on the fire-escape made me believe otherwise. But why the abduction? Ransom, as a motive, was out of the question and I couldn't think of a single soul who'd want to kill him. For what?

Cherchez the coats, Wanda said. Maybe she was on to something. I looked up at the clock on the wall. I wouldn't find anything out sitting around my damn office. The bars'll be opening soon.

I threw on my coat and reached for my keys, but they weren't where they were supposed to be. They never were. The next thirty minutes I ransacked my office, my apartment, everywhere, searching for my keys. I found them on a shelf in the refrigerator. Don't ask. Leaving the brownstone, I flashed on the idea that whatever it was that someone had been searching for in Steadwell's apartment, like my keys, had to be smaller than a breadbox—else why had they searched the dresser drawers.

First stop, Showman's—the regulars would be warming the stools and information could probably be bought for the price of a drink.

A bar seen in the daytime is a depressing sight. All the nighttime aura gone, its smells seems stronger, its customers sadder. Inside Showman's, one of the oldest and most enduring night spots in Harlem, cigarette and alcohol smells lingered in the walls and floors. Slashes of light struggled through the front window and dust motes two-stepped in the air. I stood inside the doorway and allowed my eyes to adjust to the gloom.

Two men, with early-morning beers in front of them, slouched over the bar. A woman with her ass hanging over the bar stool screeched with laughter at something one of the men said. At my approach the trio turned in tandem and the woman called to me, "Hey, Mr. Man, Mr. Man, is that you?"

I didn't know the woman from Adam, but I chickenshit grinned like I did, and she sunshined me back with a wide and welcoming smile.

"Hey, I remember you. You remember me, Mr. Man? Why don't you buy an old friend a drink?"

I wasn't fooled. The woman was hustling me for a drink, that was all. But she seemed a friendly sort, so I signaled to the bartender and threw money on the bar.

Beaming at her good luck, she turned to the men on either side of her, "Now, see, this man—he a gentleman. He know how to treat a lady. I disremember—what's your name, sugar?"

She blinked buttermilk eyes at me, and her cohorts rolled with laughter—it was the 'lady' part that set them to laughing.

"Name's Amos Brown. Looking for somebody. Maybe you seen her? Skinny. About five-four, big eyes. Name's Patty Duvall. Last seen wearing a big old mink coat."

New laughter erupted from the man on her right. He banged his empty beer bottle on the counter and belched.

I asked him if that meant that he knew Patty. He cut his eyes at me, and asked what the information was worth. Real quick I could see it would cost me more than a drink. I started with a ten.

"If the information is righteous—" I said, and held up the money.

Laughter shot out of him in short bursts like the rat-tat-tat of a down-and-dirty fart. "The skinny ones turn you on, huh?" he said.

I slid the ten back in my pocket. He noticed, swiped his mouth with his hand, and his eyes tightened. The woman piped up, "Aw hell, don't mind Bucky—Bucky don't even know what day it is—he can't tell you shit. I know who you talking 'bout. New in town— one of Dap's hookers. Works off 134th and Amsterdam. Been in here lots the past month. In here last night."

Bucky slapped the bar with his hand and whined, "Ruby, how come you can't keep your mouth shut? Giving away information for free. Sucker ain't gone pay now."

Ruby thought hard about what Bucky said and then looked back at me. "Oh, he gone pay, 'cause he a gentleman. You gone pay, ain't you, mister?"

I pulled out two tens and placed the money in front of Ruby. Ruby didn't play. She snatched the money, hoisted her rump off the stool and bumped against me, her voice low and deep. I flew backwards, rebounding off the bar and ended up chest to titty with her. Ruby wasn't a lightweight.

"What else you want, mister?" she said, almost purring.

Not none of that. Lord help. I loosened my collar and put a little distance between us. "Think I could find her there now?"

She shrugged her shoulders, disappointed her charms didn't work on me, and propped herself back up on the stool. She lapped her drink and said, "Dap Jones's stable all over the place—you know, 'cause of what happened to him—maybe she on the block, maybe no. Girls looking for a new pimp now, you know?" And then Ruby had a bright idea. "That's how come you looking for her, ain't it?"

None of her business. After all, she wasn't paying *me*.

The bartender shoved a new drink at Ruby. "Gal, ain't you the one said you fixing to turn over a new leaf just this morning, talking about getting saved? Didn't you just tell us all that? Said you was taking your butt to First A.M.E. Church today for the eleven o'clock prayer hour?"

"Hell, Marty, Jesus don't serve no refreshments," she said and tumbled liquor down her throat.

The bartender shook his head, and looked over to me. "I try," he said. "You a relative?"

I did a double take—at Ruby, and then at the bartender. Was he serious? He shook his head again. "I meant, you a relative of the girl's? I can read people pretty well. You don't look like no pimp. You trying to help her?"

Okay, I figured I was an almost relative, so I nodded. He leaned in to me.

"The girl don't look like no hooker, either. Just—in trouble, you know? See it all the time. Drugs is the problem. I do what I can to help. Girl's deep in it, I know that. Can see it in her eyes. She was in here last night, all right, looking for a guy—gave me money to point him out to her."

I gripped the bartender's arm. "Looking for who?"

"Old dude. Name of Steadwell."

I swallowed hard. The bartender's news knocked me for a loop.

"What time you see him?"

"About nine."

I tossed a couple more bills on the bar; the bartender wished me luck and I split.

Chapter 17

Steadwell wasn't dead, but he was going to be dead when I found him. Patty was the key. I hustled north, picked up a barbeque sandwich, and drove to 134th Street and Amsterdam and parked. A good minute hadn't passed before a hooker approached and offered her wares for sale. She caught me with my mouth full of barbeque, so maybe my "no" didn't sound like a "no" because she jerked open the car door and jumped in anyway.

Sister Girl with the double D's tugged at my clothes and started kissing on me while I tried to wipe barbeque sauce off my lips and at the same time fend her off with a rib bone.

No go. We got all tangled up, and even though I shouted "stop," Sister Girl went at it hard and heavy and tugged and jerked at the zipper on my pants.

Didn't the woman understand that no means no? What was wrong with her? "Patty Duvall," I screamed. Abruptly, the mauling stopped. She scooted back over to the passenger side, barbeque sauce dripping from her large lips and staining her blouse. She looked like a vampire who had just sucked off a victim. A horrible sight. I shuddered.

"Patty Duvall. Hmph, why you ain't want somebody with meat on their bones?" she said.

"It ain't about meat," I said, fingernailing the rib meat from between my teeth. "You seen her?" She crossed her arms and poked her lips out until they nearly touched the dashboard, no lie.

I pulled out a twenty and it disappeared so fast you would have thought she was a magician. Then she said, "She here last night. When her habit come down, she be back. Just wait." Then she jumped out of the car, and whammed Sugar's door shut. I cringed. "You gonna wait for her?"

"Have to."

"Well, park further down the block. You park too close, people think you the Man. I'll let her know you looking for her."

I nodded. Flipped off another ten and gave it to her, put Sugar in reverse, and backed the car down the block. Passing cars sent me New York love—honking horns, the middle finger salute and someone called me an asshole. This time when I parked I was careful to lock my doors. No more surprises.

Three o'clock rolled around, and my bladder was talking to me and my teeth were floating, but I stayed put—didn't want to take a chance on missing Patty. Finally, I couldn't take it anymore. I jumped out of the car and relieved myself against a building, the cold air giving me an instant woodie, and I had a devil of a time stuffing myself back in my pants.

Wouldn't you know it? Just then, a slight figure with arms wrapped tightly around her body, dressed in a short jacket and shorter skirt, walked rapidly past my car. I ran after her, shouting, "Patty."

She stopped and turned.

I held the coat closed. "We need to talk," I said. "I've been waiting for you." She looked as if she might break and run, and then she changed her mind and nodded, and let me lead her back to the car. I opened the door on the passenger side and Patty, shivering, slid in. I circled behind the car, finished zippering, and when I joined her she wouldn't look me in the eye. After being caught with my fly open I had a hard time looking at her too.

"Where's your fur coat? You need something heavier than what you got on."

Patty's face was drawn and tight. She moved away and stared stonily out of the window.

"Okay, listen," I said, "I'm hungry. Let's go get us something to eat, some soup or something? How about it? It'll warm you up."

Patty bobbed her head yes, and I switched on the engine. During the trip, Patty's body shook and she didn't say a word. Sugar rolled us to Lenox Avenue and I pulled up to Denise's, a soul food restaurant with a good menu and Christian sentiment championed on a sign above the door, IN GOD WE TRUST. The street element never hung out here and that was good. I hoped to avoid gossip.

Lunch hour had passed. Inside the restaurant only a few patrons occupied tables. I settled Patty in, we ordered, and I watched while Patty slurped her soup. After she began to look human once more, I asked again. "What happened to your coat?"

She shrugged her shoulders.

"Look, girl, I ain't asking for the sake of conversation—I need to know about that coat."

"Hocked it," she said.

"Why?"

Patty's tongue shot from her mouth like a sea serpent and she licked her lips. "For the money—why else you think?"

"Tricking ain't paying your bills?"

"Not since Dap."

I leaned forward. "You get that coat from Dap?"

"I fount it."

I'd heard that before and I wasn't having it. I grabbed her wrist. "Found it, my ass. You stole it from Dap. Was that before or after he was murdered?"

Frightened eyes stared back at me. She struggled to break the iron grip I had on her. Strong-arming women wasn't my style so I released her.

"Look, Patty, if you haven't figured it out by now—I'm trying to help, but you're not making it easy."

Her body shook as if she were having a seizure. "I got to get back my baby—I needed the money." Copious tears fell while she jerked and twitched. Crack cocaine did awful things.

"Hold on, just hold on," I urged.

I guess the waitress lounging at the counter mistook me for

Patty's pimp because she threw me a hard look. Her boss, Denise, wasn't there to vouch for me and I had to fend for myself. Indignant, I returned her looks and checked her out the same way she was checking me. Her nostrils quivered and she massaged the bunions on her feet, disapproval heavy on her face. We had a stare-down, until vanquished, she at last turned away.

I leaned into Patty. "Did you kill him?"

"Who you talking 'bout?"

"Dap," I said. "Did you kill him?"

This time her eyes rounded into perfect zeros. "No, Mr. Brown, no. Dap already dead when I got there."

"You were at his apartment?" She nodded. "The coats were still there?"

"No. Gone, 'cept for one."

My skepticism evident, she stammered and said, "Honest to God. The rack was standing there empty. I looked through his stuff, checked out his closet, and found a coat—hidden way in the back. So I took it. I figured Dap didn't need it no more."

Sensible. "You were looking for Steadwell. Why?"

"Everyone knew about the coats being stolen from him and people afraid to buy it from me. I tried to sell it, but couldn't get any money for it. Then I thought Steadwell might give me some money if I gave it back to him."

"Three times stolen. That coat has more legs than a centipede. Where is Steadwell?"

Patty raised her shoulders again. Before they dropped into a shrug again I squeezed her hand. "Ow, Mr. Brown, leggo. I ain't never seen him."

"Where's the coat?"

"Pawnshop. Bunky give me something on it."

Patty pulled some money from the bodice of her dress and pushed crumpled bills at me, along with a pawn ticket. "You keep it—for Josephine."

"Josephine doesn't need your money. She's being taken care of."

"No, she ain't. I seen him. I seen him, Mr. Brown. I know what's going on. He got the mark, Wilbur does. Man ain't going to last.

That's why he mad at me. 'Cause I know he ain't going to be around, and there ain't going to be nobody around to take care of my baby." Then she broke down for real and cried. I let her. The waitress rolled bowling ball eyes my way.

"I got to get myself together. Would you hold this money for me, Mr. Brown? 'Fore I mess it up. When I get straight I be back for it. If I don't come back, give it to my baby. Please, keep it for me, Mr. Brown."

I counted the money. Two hundred dollars. Bunky had ripped her off. I banded the bills and the pawn ticket in with my money and stuck the roll back in my pocket. That was the nail on the coffin, the evidence the waitress needed. She hobbled to our table as fast as her bunion feet could carry her. On the pretext of refilling my cup, she sloshed hot coffee in my lap.

Jesus. I scrambled backward. If my reflexes had been any slower, you would have seen boiled dick on the menu. The waitress sucked her teeth and snarled, "Sorry," and walked away.

Dabbing at my pants, I scowled and said to Patty, "You finished? Let's get out of here." And then I had a thought. "Why would Dap hide one of the coats in the back of his closet?"

"Probably saving it to give to his number one."

"His number one? Who'd that be?"

"I wasn't introduced. I just heard Dap say her name. Charlize Somebody—"

My eyes bucked and I knocked the coffee cup over, burning my own damn self. The waitress at the far end of the counter orgasmed, she was so happy.

How many Charlizes could there be in Harlem? "Charlize, you said? Are you sure? Charlize—with big titties?"

In slow drips the coffee puddled on the floor. The waitress arrived in time for next Christmas and made a limp pass over the table with her rag, her sneer plastered to her sin ugly face. Could a brother catch a break?

I'd had it. I threw money on the table, no tip for this waitress. "Let's go, Patty."

Patty squeaked, "Bigger'n mine."

"What?" I had forgotten my question.

"Bigger'n mine. Her titties are bigger'n mine," she repeated.

I surveyed Patty's chest, so did the waitress. Anybody's tits would be bigger than Patty's. Two fleas lunching on a picnic table. With both of us staring, Patty grabbed her bag, and locked her arms across her chest.

We left the restaurant, my mind racing. Outside, day had turned to night. Charlize hooking for Dap? Naww . . . not possible. Had to be a mistake.

As if she were reading my mind, Patty said, "Charlize wasn't never on the block, but I think she be hooking for him, sure enough."

Somebody like Charlize would have Dap on a leash, not the other way around. No, I couldn't see it.

While walking to the car, I said, "You know somebody name of Hazel—works for Poontang Wanda?"

Patty shook her head. Of course she didn't. She and Hazel were in two different worlds. "Anybody else you know sporting one of the missing coats?"

Another blank wall.

At the car I said, "Where you sleeping tonight?"

When Patty didn't answer, I figured she didn't have a place. Against my better judgment I made her an offer. "You can stay in a room in one of my buildings—the one across the street—for a couple of days. It's got a bed, dresser, and the basics in it—but you have to keep that crack shit off my property and off my street. You fuck up, you're gone. I got your money, I'll keep it as a deposit. You mess up, I keep it, period. Next few days, if you make up your mind to get some help, I'll see that you get it."

Patty stared at me, and then she broke down again for the second time that night. I looked away. Then she slowly nodded her head. "Got to do what I need to do to get my baby back."

"Look, I'll be straight with you—I don't know if that's going to happen. But at least you'll be near her, for a little while, anyway. Do we have a deal?"

She nodded her head again.

I dropped her off at home and squared her away. Light drifts of snow were beginning to fall. Yesterday's warm spell had disappeared like a whim and today the extreme cold had chased most people indoors. I pulled a twenty-five pound bag of rock salt out from the basement and sprinkled the sidewalk and stairs in front of both brownstones. Tomorrow the trash would be picked up and Seltzer would handle the cans. I bent to retrieve the nearly empty bag of salt.

Three pops from a gun shattered the quiet of the night, and I dove to the pavement and ate salt—the noise familiar, my reaction instinctive. Someone screamed across the street. I spit salt out of my mouth and looked around, searching for the shooter. People came out of their homes, fools rushing to a fire. Across the street my neighbor looked up. I mimicked his look and scanned the rooftops but could see nothing. I rose and brushed clumps of snow off my pants. I had scraped my hand and a trickle of blood ran down my arm and on to my pants. Perfect.

Where had the shots come from and for whom were they intended? Nobody seemed to be hurt, and people resumed what they were doing.

A neighbor waved and yelled, "Ain't nobody safe anymore."

"Probably some junior hoodlum taking potshots for target practice," I said.

"Or somebody's dead behind a door," he offered.

I shook my head. Living in the Wild West wasn't easy. I waved back to my neighbor and picked up the bag of salt, once again. That's when I noticed the garbage can. I bent to look. Two bullet holes had been ripped into the side of one of the cans. I froze.

Some kid playing with a gun? Or had I been the intended target? I quickly looked up again and around me. Nothing stirred. Anyway, who the hell would want to kill me?

Inside my office, I dumped the bag of salt in a corner and retrieved the .38 again from the filing cabinet. It's not like I was unaccustomed to hearing gunshots up in Harlem, but to have bullets aimed at me—that was a different thing. Could have been pranksters, or maybe that kid from the other night, but I wasn't taking chances and I wasn't going to be caught unprepared.

I had another stop to make before I'd call it quits for the night. Trembling with fatigue, but loaded for bear this time, I carried the bulky gun with me and cruised over to Wells'. Still no Sergio. No Italians at all. What was he, a phantom? I hung around the place until I couldn't keep my eyes open any longer. I consumed a large portion of Wells' chicken and waffles and nodded out like any junkie, I was that tired. I stumbled to my car and headed home.

That night I slept with the .38 under my pillow—a lumpy night.

Chapter 18

The day of Harry's funeral I arose with the tweeters. Anticipation at seeing Catherine had me trembling like a chihuahua.
At least that was what I thought. Maybe I trembled in fear of a
speeding bullet ripping a hole through my underwear.

I changed clothes twice, made three trips to my car—twice without her present—and the last time, with it, sweating goblets, even
though outside the weather was colder than a meat locker. I carried
my smaller piece, a .25, strapped to my ankle.

Climbing into Sugar, frost blew out of my mouth, but my palms
were damp and under my hat sweat cha-cha'ed in trickles down my
forehead. I took off my gloves and drove bare-knuckled to Buster's
Heavenly Rest Funeral Home on Eighth Avenue.

When I arrived, cars were double-parked up and down the block.
Harry the Monkey Chaser's funeral was a Harlem Event. The criminal element was out in force, along with representatives of the police department. Harlem society and Harlem's underbelly brushed
shoulders and meeted and greeted like old friends. Buster, solemn in
black, stood in front directing cars away from the entrance. A battal-
ion of Black Muslims stood guard at the crowd's perimeter, stone-
faced and rigid, their presence probably a good thing.

Me, I stayed on the lookout for whoever was looking for me, and
maybe for the sighting of a fur or two. On this occasion I wasn't

disappointed. It was a furrier's convention, there were so many, and now the idea of cherchez-les-furs didn't seem so hot.

People clustered on the sidewalk and bodies overflowed into the street. Incredible. Harry, Harlem's favorite son? True, Harry had regularly contributed to the community, but everyone knew that it was to keep the wheels well-greased in his favor. Damn, but people had short memories. Me included. Four years ago, Harry was looking to kill me. But at Harry's funeral, it was let bygones be bygones. I surveyed the scene. Tucked among the gentlefolk were the hard-asses, friends as well as enemies of Harry—magnets, repelling each other and traveling in packs.

Although Buster's Heavenly Rest was by far the largest funeral home in Harlem, it'd never accommodate this crowd. Some people would be standing in the cold. Too bad Harry was an atheist. Some of the largest African-American churches in the entire country were located in the village of Harlem, and Harry could have had his funeral in any one of them. For sure Catherine hadn't anticipated this many—and what a odiferous group they were.

Caught in a crush of people, I was nearly asphyxiated as heat rose from the multitudes and wave after wave of perfume, cologne, and aftershave almost overcame me. I had to hold my breath as I pushed my way up to the door of the chapel, no easy task.

At the entrance, Catherine stood in a emerald suit, a mocha beauty sandwiched between two of Harry's goons, shaking people's hands and greeting them. She saw me and waved, and motioned to Harry's men to let me come through.

Suddenly, Prince appeared at my elbow and crowded in behind me, indicating to the goons that he was with me. I conceded and pushed him ahead of me and pecked Catherine on the cheek—neither the time nor place for anything else—and Prince and I moved into the chapel. Of course, he instantly disappeared—working the crowd, no doubt.

Inside, I slapped a few hands, and let myself be thumped and patted on the back in return. To a trusted few I dropped the news about Steadwell. They gave me troubled looks—nobody held out much hope for his return, but I told them to get in touch with me in case they saw him.

Through swirls of bodies I spotted Wanda, shining like a copper penny, dressed in a glittery number that moved with her great hips as she walked. On her head she wore an amazing hat with a large and dangerous feather. At each turn of her head, people darted and dipped around her.

She saw me, too, and came over and slipped me a piece of paper and whispered, "On Tuesday—that Evinrude guy'll be at his Manhattan apartment. Hazel's having dinner with him at seven. Be careful."

"Oh, I'll be careful. Somebody's trying to kill me." Wanda looked up, startled. I pocketed the paper and she moved reluctantly away from me, the waves of people parting for her. Wanda commanded a lot of respect.

McGillihand was there with his buddies from the Police Athletic League—Harry had been a donor, thanks to me—and I shot the shit with them while hugging and slapping five with friends and acquaintances. Old home week at the funeral—hardly anyone there that I didn't know or know of. Harlem Village wasn't that big, and occasions like this proved it.

The music sounded; social amenities aside, it was time to begin. Some people had forgotten why they were here, networking the order of the day. The ushers had a devil of a time trying to get people to move into the chapel. Swear to God, one man pulled out his gun to get to his business cards and no one standing nearby had the slightest reaction, not even the woman whom he asked to hold his gun.

I made my way to a pew near the front, not too far from Catherine, and plopped down one seat over from a familiar face. Oh no, not Basil . . . Soldiers from Harry's drug army flanked him to the right and left and front and back, artillery bulging under their dark suits.

Basil had told me he expected something to go down at Harry's funeral. I looked around. Whoever wanted to take him out, I hoped to God they could shoot straight. Sitting way too close to the bull's-eye. I shifted in my seat, gripped my ankle and touched my own piece for comfort.

A large man entered the pew and wriggled into the space on my left, and I was wedged between him on the left and Basil's man on the right. I turned to take him in. Jesus. Sumo George, Harry's former stooge. Wasn't he supposed to be doing twenty-five-to-life? When did he get out of jail? He grinned a toothless smile, and I shrank back into my seat. What happened to his teeth? It was then I realized it wasn't George at all—it was his cousin Louie. As if that made me feel better. I figured it wasn't by accident that he chose the seat next to mine.

Basil stared straight ahead. The organist's hands and feet hit the instrument with an earsplitting chord and the crowd silenced. Let the games begin.

Laid out in his coffin in a formal morning coat, Harry also wore a striped cravat—the works. I grimaced. Were we burying royalty here? The organist played "Shall We Gather at the River," and Basil leaned over to me and whispered.

"Like the coffin?"

I stared. Was that a question or an threat? You couldn't be sure with Basil.

"Nice," I said.

He leaned again. "See the angels carved in the side of the box?"

I pitched my body forward and squinted. The coffin's design was appropriate to Harry's extraordinarily bad taste, but you could see it was expensive, made of burnished cherry wood and inlaid ivory. The gold handles and dancing cherubim? Excessive. The tiny angels hovered around Harry's head.

"Uh-huh," I said.

"Harry wanted an escort of angels on his journey. Not my taste, but Harry picked it out ten years ago," Basil said. Then he added, "Harry believed in angels."

I knew better. Harry believed in voodoo. The organ crescendoed, and Basil waited for an interval of silence before he made his point.

"Angels. You got one watching over you—in case you didn't know it. But keep asking the wrong questions, and your angel won't be able to help you."

The squawk of a microphone prevented me from responding to Basil. Good thing. Catherine's voice coming from the front of the chapel swept over the room. She bent over the mike, made a few remarks, and thanked people for coming to her uncle's funeral. She ended with, "Let us pray." A good idea for everyone here.

I bowed and my fellow heathens did the same, but all of us peeked and caught each other looking. Then, under the big top, the circus began. A singer with healthy lungs blasted out the hymn "In the Sweet Bye and Bye" with enough volume to raise the dead. No use—Harry wasn't budging.

Testifying came next. Then some preaching, a eulogy, more testifying. Manure covered the entire chapel and the smell floated up to heaven. On my left, Louie sniffed. Then he sniffed some more. I checked my armpits, and then I checked Louie. Crocodile tears floated down his face and he acted as though he were really going to miss Harry. I handed him my handkerchief and he blubbered loudly into it. Heads turned. After a few minutes, Louie composed himself and pushed the handkerchief back to me.

I told him to keep it.

But the pretenders to Harry's throne sat in rat packs around the chapel, and I surmised that the firepower under this chapel's roof could blow away Jesus, the twelve apostles and any multitude that followed them. To say I was uneasy was an understatement, last night still on my mind. Had one of Basil's men shot at me?

I surreptitiously eyeballed Basil, and at the same time caught a glimpse of someone who resembled Steadwell standing along the far wall. I stretched to get a good look, but the figure vanished. My God. Had my lying eyes deceived me? Had it been Steadwell? I twisted my head to look around the room, searching the wall, the pews, the rear of the chapel, but no luck.

Curious, Basil followed my look. I quickly faced front. Had I only wished Steadwell here—my imagination working overtime? Blood pulsed along a vein in my forehead.

Mourners filed by, mouths hung open, viewing Harry's body and confirming that he was indeed dead. King Harry, feared and revered by all, in the end, a mortal like everybody else.

And then I had a moment.

I wasn't the only one.

Big Mobile—Big Mo', they called him—stepped out of the viewing line and rolled over to Basil. Basil's men rose in one breath, hands inside jackets. People sucked air in one loud gasp and the hairs on the back of my neck saluted the domed ceiling.

Big Mo' stalled where he stood and surrendered his hands in the air. Then he slowly extended a hand across the pews in the offer of a handshake. When Basil accepted his handshake the crowd exhaled, and Basil's henches took their seats.

Mo' knocked knuckles with Basil and said, "Ah'm witch you, man." That was all he said but that was enough for me, and I looked to see if it was enough to satisfy Basil. It was. Mo's action started a trend, and the pledge of allegiance was offered at least ten more times by various gangster types. Basil acknowledged each with a nod and a handshake. Basil was in—the transition of power taking place at Harry's funeral, and the threat of a drug war was eradicated.

The preacher quickly tossed out a benediction, amen-ed one last time, and the charade was over. Basil turned to me but I excused myself and quickly moved to the front row where Mrs. Walters, Harry's sister, sat. She looked up at me, eyes wet and nose runny. "Him trash, I know, but him me brother and I'll miss him, I will."

I took her hands in mine and sat with her. People offered condolences to Mrs. Walters and Catherine, to the many cousins, nephews and assorted members of Harry's family and organization. Catherine sat quietly. She didn't watch when six of Harry's men, now Basil's, lifted Harry's casket on their shoulders and bore him out of the chapel to the waiting hearse.

I helped Mrs. Walters up, and we followed Catherine up the aisle and out of doors to the waiting limousine. After I settled the old woman in the car, and turned back to say something to Catherine, on its own my heart scudded to the bottom of my feet, bounced back up, and stuck in my throat. I couldn't utter a word.

I stuttered, but couldn't get anything out. The gift I had bought for her waited in my car, but I knew it had been a stupid idea to bring it and my face burned red. To a funeral? What had I been thinking?

Someone thumped me on my shoulder. Prince. Not again. He lunged past me to take Catherine's hand.

"Amos didn't introduce us before. My name is Prince. You helped with the senator's campaign, didn't you? And I've also seen you at Abyssinian Church. I'm pleased to finally meet you and I'm sorry about your loss."

I coughed to remind Prince I was there.

"Uh, Prince Higgans, Esquire. Meet Catherine Walters."

Catherine looked to me. Hell, this wasn't my idea. I said, "Prince here is my lawyer—uh, Steadwell's, that is, a friend of mine's lawyer. Well, I hired him, but—"

Catherine looked even more confused. "Steadwell? Who's Steadwell?"

"Uh, nobody you'd know."

Catherine arched an eyebrow and I knew what that meant—she categorized Steadwell immediately as one of my hoodlum friends, a lot of nerve for a drug lord's niece. The woman had a *lot* of nerve. She hadn't said anything, but I was mad. Prince still held her hand and was not letting go.

He said, "I'm running for city council and I'd like to talk to you sometime." A buzzing started in my ears. Coming from where? Buzz, buzz. Like a cyclone of bees, Prince swarmed Catherine. Surprise and delight flitted across Catherine's face. She opened like a morning glory under his flattering words and he fingered her petals, stinger ready, as my face flamed.

"Where's Charlize?" I asked, interrupting.

But Prince had orbited out of the universe and barely heard me. "Who?" he said.

"Your secretary, Charlize."

"Oh, Charlize. She had to take care of office things. Business."

Prince off his leash and this was the result? Catherine and Prince danced some more, and they didn't use their feet. Three-hundred-sixty degrees of mutuality was established in less than five minutes. For God's sake, this at Harry's funeral. Had they no shame?

Hustling through the crowd, over Prince's shoulder I saw Basil making his way toward me. Not good. Catherine's mother lowered the limo window and called, "Me brother rolling in the ground and them throwing dirt in his face, and we ain't there to see him go. Hurry up, gal. Get along, Amos. See you at the cemetery."

As if the delay were my fault.

Prince Fucking Charming helped Catherine in and shut the door, his riney head still in conversation with Catherine. It was too much. I thumped the hood and signaled the driver to go, and he pulled away with a piece of Prince's ear.

Not ten feet away, Basil pressed toward me. I pretended not to see him signaling me and thanked God for the crowd. I flapped my wings and flew straight to my car, leaving Prince holding a bleeding ear and looking distressed. Somebody called to wait up, but I wasn't stopping. Besides, I'd wind up knocking Prince flat on his ass, and then the Muslim brothers would jump me or Basil might kill me. No, better to keep walking. Sic Charlize on Prince—that'd fix him.

I wrenched open my car door and hopped in. Prince and Basil were deep in conversation. I stared, drumming my fingers on the steering wheel. Prince was the first to turn and glance at me, but Basil didn't seem interested at all and kept his attention on Prince.

A cortege formed as cars folded into a procession and trailed Harry's hearse up the avenue. I turned over Sugar's engine and headed in the opposite direction. Mrs. Walters I'd see later. For now, I'd go home, lick my wounds, eat raw meat, and pretend I was munching on Prince.

I had driven a few blocks when, in my rearview mirror, I saw a figure slip between two parked cars and head east. I braked, tore out of my car, and sprinted after him. People stared as I pounded past and then pulled up short at the corner. Had I lost him? I turned the corner but the figure had disappeared. I circled around myself like a dog chasing its tail. No use. Steadwell had vanished.

Chapter 19

Parked in front of my brownstone, I saw Miss Ellie, my oldest tenant, trudging through the snow in too-high heels and lugging a bag of groceries. Crazy lady. I locked Sugar up tight, tucked Catherine's present under my arm and crossed the street.

Miss Ellie had danced at the Cotton Club in its heyday, and always dazzled me with the stories about the celebrities she hung out with and the high jinks she was guilty of in the glory days of her youth. Age hadn't diminished her beauty. She was still a good-looking woman, with nicely shaped calves, and a petite, curvaceous frame that made even younger men do a turnabout. In her eighties she rebuffed the geriatric set and socialized with the forty- or fifty-year-olds, with whom she often flirted and kept company.

The sight of her restored me to some sanity. I smiled, and lifted the burden from her arms.

"Why are you carrying this? No old flame around to help you?"

"Honey, all my old flames got their lights extinguished. They won't be carrying no bags today."

"Saying they're all dead?"

"As a doornail. Got whiskey here, Amos. Care to join a lady for a drink?"

Well, hell, why not? Recrimination, anger, sadness, and a touch of fear had been dancing on my shoulders all week. What better way to unwind than chug a drink or two with Miss Ellie? The woman made me laugh, and anyway, I had time to kill before I headed over to Mrs. Walters's home, so I told Miss Ellie I'd be honored to have a drink with her in celebration of the holidays.

"The holidays? What's the holidays got to do with it? Didn't we hoist a couple a few weeks ago, and didn't I drink you under the table?"

I blushed and admitted that she did. "Thanksgiving weekend. A holiday."

"Is that a fact? Amos, ain't you got a girlfriend? How come you hanging with an old lady on holidays?"

What'd she have to say that for? I deflected it with, "What old lady? You see an old lady somewhere?"

Miss Ellie snorted and said, "God made a simpleton and named him Amos. Child, you ain't got a bit of sense and that's the truth."

"Sense enough to know I'm drinking with one fine mama—now what you got to say to that?"

Her face creased into a smile. "I say—what you got under your arm?" She pointed to Catherine's boxed dress.

I considered the package. "Looks like a present, don't it? For one fine mama."

Miss Ellie brightened and her joy was touching to see. "Why, Amos. You remembered my birthday? If you aren't the sweetest landlord. I never remembered telling you my birthday came after Christmas. Since it comes so close to Christmas, most people forget it."

I couldn't flimflam an old lady. "Sorry, Miss Ellie, I didn't remember—no, I didn't remember at all. This present—well, let's just say, it never got delivered."

Miss Ellie regarded me intently. Then she took the box out of my hands. "Well, it doesn't matter. We'll just call it delivered and I'm pleased as punch to get it. Now, let's have that drink."

I smiled and we entered the brownstone and I followed her upstairs to her place. Inside her apartment she broke out the glasses and put Duke Ellington 78 records on an ancient phonograph, and we had a rip-roaring afternoon. She roared and I got ripped.

Chapter 20

All good things must come to an end. Before six o'clock, just short of blind drunk, I left Miss Ellie's place and stood in the December chill outside the iron gate in front of my residence, struggling to pull myself together. My orbs felt as if they belonged to somebody else and they rolled in my head like loose marbles. The snow-covered landscape undulated in waves around me. Jesus, I needed coffee—I was in no shape to go calling on anybody, let alone Mrs. Walters, that tough old bird.

A few stumbles and I made it up the steps and into my apartment. How does it happen? That woman does it to me every time. *That's right, blame an old woman, asshole.*

In my tiny kitchen I didn't bother to measure the coffee and dumped water and coffee grounds into Mr. Coffee, then laid my head on the counter to listen to the water gurgle, which sounded like a man drowning. Was I drowning? Lulled by the gurgle, I must have slept for a time because when I opened my eyes the sounds had stopped and Mr. Coffee's pot was full. I peeled my cheek off the sink, shrugged out of my coat and jacket and flung the clothes in front of me into the living room, following behind them like Mary's Little Lamb.

In the living room I belched so hard that I grabbed my belly and acrid gas hissed across the room. Some days it's chicken, some days, feathers. Another belch and then sublime release. I aimed my body at the couch and fell face first into it. A church bell tolled six gongs faintly and the lyrics of an old television commercial ran loops around my brain. *Six o'clock, dinner time, too late to make dessert.* Crash.

Two hours later, the smell of scorched coffee and the dribble of my saliva woke me up. And whaddaya know? Insight made a home in my head—as comfortable as a visiting relative at Christmas. Understanding dawned and I suddenly knew some things.

I knew Catherine was a lost cause. And I was positive it'd been Steadwell that I'd seen at Harry's funeral, that it hadn't been a hallucination. But what was with his disappearing act, for Christ's sake? Nose bent against the cushions, I struggled to breathe and forced myself up off the couch.

And Basil had something brewing. The last was still a mystery. In the middle of nothing, a monster's hand reached inside my chest and wrenched my heart, squeezing and twisting it so tightly that I gasped from the pain. What the fuck? Emotions threatened to spill over. What was going on here? I took a couple of deep breaths. The holidays, love and cha-cha-cha. A lot of people get depressed this time of year. Whatever. *Man, you better stop drinking*.

I got up, took a quick shower, brushed my teeth until my gums bled, doused Listerine down my throat, then threw on casual slacks and a shirt, an aqua number with yellow surprises splashed over it. I should call somebody. Elise? Lightweight conversationalist, but not bad-looking. Well, hell, I wasn't going to discuss physics with her—the faster we hit the sheets, the better. I went to my phone-book and searched for her number, starting with the A's. Dammit, what was her last name?

While flipping pages, I happened on another name. Bess Tanner. I jumped up. Steadwell's old girlfriend. He had once given me her number. Bess and Steadwell had been on again, off again, for years and he stayed at her place for months at a time. I got excited. Hell, the man might be holed up with her even now. Bess lived in a building off 110th Street, just above Central Park. Eight o'clock. What happened to the time? Forget Elise—I had to hurry. I'd go by for a quick visit with Mrs. Walters and then drop by Bess's.

But first—

I dashed to the kitchen and poured myself a cup of hot coffee, guzzled it, and burned the shit out of my tongue. That sobered me.

I stepped over the clothes I had left in the middle of the living room floor, had a second thought and retrieved the scrap of paper from my jacket pocket, grabbed my overcoat, and weathered up once more. Hurrying outside, the night air cut into me like knives, but the sky was bright with stars. Heaven's eyes beamed down and I stepped under a halo of light and a rush of warmth surged through me. Something touched my shoulder—as if an angel had lit there. I held my shoulder and looked up into the glimmering night. Well, somebody was on my side.

Mrs. Walters sat, one hand curled on her lap, lightly dozing by the fireplace. Catherine had let me in. I should have known she'd be there. We exchanged the briefest of words. I moved quietly to the couch opposite the old woman's chair and waited. Her eyelids fluttered as she pulled herself upright and wiped a hand across her mouth.

"Amos, why you ain't follow us to the cemetery?"

I lied. "An emergency. Something came up with a tenant."

"Food's put away."

"I don't need anything to eat."

Mrs. Walters barked at Catherine, standing nearby. "Girl, what you waiting for? Him hungry, no doubt about it. Fix the man a plate."

Throwing a look at both of us, Catherine didn't protest and headed off to the kitchen. I followed her exit with my eyes. My crotch warmed and I crossed my legs. Her mother gripped my arm and caught me off balance and off guard. My whole body tipped over and I crashed to the floor. Mrs. Walters glared and said, "Amos, I need your help, ain't no time for foolishness."

"What is it?" I said, sitting cross-legged on the floor.

She struggled up from her rocking chair and hurried over to a large secretary. She lifted a leather portfolio out of a drawer and riffled through its contents and pulled out a sheaf of papers.

"Read," she said.

Her urgency prompted me and I read as she ordered.

"I, Harry Algonquin Bridges, being of sound mind . . ." Good God, it was Harry's will.

"No, no time, skip to page seven."

I read where she indicated. The gist was that Harry had left most of his fortune to Catherine, including the lavender-colored mansion in Englewood, New Jersey.

"Harry's burden left on Catherine's shoulders. Awful. Awful."

Me, I didn't see what was so awful. "Mrs. Walters, your daughter is going to be rich woman."

"Evil money. Bad money."

I shrugged. "Well, there's that, but Catherine didn't have anything to do with how Harry made his living."

A small wail burst from her. "Its evil will destroy her. Already people are after her." Mrs. Walters wrung her hands together.

I said, "Catherine can handle them."

"Phone calls, all the time, from people she don't know and from some she do. The calls are not so nice. Especially from me grand-nephew."

"Who's your grand-nephew?"

Mrs. Walters sucked her teeth and spat out, "Basil. Him say me brother's house belong to organization and Harry meant for him to have it."

I indicated the will. "Obviously, Harry's will says differently. There's nothing Basil can do."

"Secrets in that house. Harry's men are still in there."

"They've taken over the house?"

Mrs. Walters nodded.

"Catherine needs to get a lawyer." Even as I said the word *lawyer*, Prince's face leapt to mind.

"Her needs protection."

"That, too."

Mrs. Walters raised her eyebrows, the question big as day in the middle of her forehead. "You talk to Basil."

"Oh, no, I can't—"

Catherine's entrance cut off my objections. She had returned with a tray and a plate stacked high with smothered chicken and mashed potatoes, mac and cheese, collard greens, cornbread—you name it.

"I can't—" I repeated and plowed into the food. When I came up for air, both Catherine and Mrs. Walters were smiling at me. That wasn't good.

The look on Mrs. Walters's face told me my commitment to her and her daughter was a done deal. I blinked. I hoped that angel was still on my shoulder.

Chapter 21

I was rooted inside a chimney with bricks stacked around me. They were being mortared in place, and I stood there doing nothing as, brick by brick, I was entombed. Helpless, that's how I felt as I buzzed Bess Tanner's building. The front door clicked open. No intercom? I pushed through the entrance before the door changed its mind and rode the elevator up to Bess's apartment on the twenty-sixth floor.

When the elevator doors parted, a sixty-something woman with unlikely red hair stuck her head out of a doorway at the end of the hall. Before I could reach the head, the head spoke, "He ain't here."

"Bess, you may not remember me—"

"I remember you, and he ain't here."

"Okay, but you've seen him, haven't you?"

She breathed heavily and a tuft of hair lifted off her forehead. I persisted. "Did Steadwell leave the coats with you?"

"What coats?" she said.

"The fur coats. Steadwell didn't tell you about them?"

"The coats that were stolen from him?"

"Yeah, well, looks like they may have been stolen again."

"I don't know nothing about nothing."

"Look, is Steadwell staying with you or not?"

Silence. Zippo. Didn't invite me in to her apartment. Was Steadwell hiding inside?

I tried again. "Steadwell's got to show up in court Tuesday. If he doesn't, it's my ass. Can I check inside?"

Her lips were zipped tighter than the corset she wore. I gave up. "All right. When you see him, remind him that I did him a favor. Tuesday, nine A.M. Tell him to call me." I turned to go.

She called after me, mouth pulled down in a frown. "Don't expect to see him. Gone underground, he said, and he ain't going to see me no more. Say if I need to get a message to him, get in touch with the Sidewinder."

"Where can I find this Sidewinder?"

"Sidewinder hangs out in Riverside Park, around 79th street."

"What's he look like?"

Arms crossed, she shrugged. "Who you asking?"

"All right. Be careful who you buzz in. Other folks might be looking for Steadwell."

"I ain't stupid. Camera in the lobby works. I knew it was you."

With that, Miss Congeniality disappeared into her apartment and slammed the door.

Uh-huh.

The sun had disappeared. Hunched on a bench in Riverside Park for the past two hours, I didn't see Sidewinder, or anybody who looked like they'd wind to the side. Pedestrians pushed against the brutal wind that had kicked up in the last twenty minutes. Small branches snapped off of trees and refuse bounced and swirled along the ground. My legs had turned to blocks of ice and my teeth chattered, so I stood up and moved around, stamping my feet and pacing back and forth.

For the last two hours I had accosted homeless people and asked them if they'd seen Steadwell or the man called Sidewinder. Mostly they'd scuttle away at my approach, like prehistoric cockroaches, scurrying down the paths that wound through the park in search of shelter. The bold ones hit me up for loose change.

Night had squeezed out what daylight was left. Now the destitute outnumbered the civilians and it wasn't safe to stay here, so I decided I'd better cut the park loose. My car was parked six blocks away.

What the hell. I checked my watch: a little before ten. Time enough to make a last stop and call it a night. But cold had settled into my bones and I needed a cup of coffee. I fingered the paper in my pocket with Hazel's boyfriend's address on it. I took it out and looked at it. Ralphie. Ralphie Evinrude. Whistling "What's It All About, Ralphie," I crossed Columbus Avenue and walked over to Broadway, ordered coffee at a coffee shop, and held my fingers over the cup to warm myself up. It took two cups to unthaw me, and then I finally headed down Broadway to 76th Street.

The doorman at Evinrude's building was busy. Standing across the street, I watched him help tenants carry packages and other assorted burdens inside. I waited, my body a washing machine, agitating in the cold. I paid attention to the traffic patterns of the people. The doorman would disappear within the building for minutes at a time, probably waiting for an elevator. Where were the stairs? Logic should tell me, but Logic didn't open his mouth.

When the doorman next disappeared into the building he was following a young woman with lots of packages and two frisky pooches. I quickly crossed the street and entered the building. Straight ahead of me was a sign that said, *Stairs*. I turned right into a small alcove that contained mail slots, a bulletin board, an intercom system and what seemed to be the doorman's station.

Quickly I searched for Evinrude's name on the mail cubbies, but they were arranged by room numbers, dammit. Underneath the counter, next to a telephone, I saw a leather bound folder and I pulled it out. The names of the tenants, their apartments and phone extensions were listed. I scanned the list quickly. Thank God for alphabetical order. 16C. An elevator pinged.

With any luck—. I dove my hand into the mail slot marked 16C and it was just as I had figured, Ralphie had left a set of spare keys. Perfect. I slipped them in my pocket and scurried out of the building.

Feeling lucky, on a hummer, I decided to head back to Riverside Park. I buttoned my coat up to the top and jammed my hands into my pockets. I looked around. The wind seemed to have picked up even more. I accelerated to a brisk pace. Brisk, shit, I practically ran back to the park.

I spied the Sidewinder immediately. About my size, his whole body listed heavily to one side. From an injury? The shopping cart he pushed had lost a wheel, and it squeaked as he steered it down the path. "Hey," I called, and chased after him. "Sidewinder?"

He turned, flight or fright etched on his face, and he pulled an object off the top of his cart, his intention clear.

I stopped in my tracks and held out a hand. "Easy, take it easy, partner," I said. "I'm looking for a friend—name of Steadwell. His lady friend told me you knew where to find him."

Sidewinder cut at me with the object, swinging it wildly in front of my face. He yelled, "Cut a worm in half, both sides wiggle. Watch out for the worm, watch out for the worm."

Oh, man, a nut job.

"Name's Amos Brown. Look, I'm his friend—Steadwell would want you to take me to him."

I stepped under the light from a street lamp to let him take a good look at me, confident I had an honest-looking face. He backed up further. Okay, so much for the honest face. When I reached for my wallet, that seemed to terrify him more than ever and he got agitated. He threw the object—the broken base of a lamp. I ducked but it nicked my shoulder.

"Shit, that hurt. What the hell is the matter with you? I'm not going to hurt you." I took a step closer, something going on with his eyes. They didn't match and one was cockeyed. "Whoa, partner. Take it easy, just getting out some money here. You can use money, can't you?"

One of his eyes was focused on the moon. The other? I glanced around to see where else he could be looking. Could the brother even see? Was he called Sidewinder because of his walk or because of his eye?

I held out a five-dollar bill. He approached cautiously and sniffed the bill, and then moved even closer and waved his hands around. This time it was me that edged backwards.

"Reading your aura," he said, his manner not as crazy as before.

"Say what?"

"Follow me."

Wasn't really sure what had happened, but I returned my money to my pocket and trekked after him, following this Quasimodo down a path to the lower level of the park, estimating that if it came to it, I could take him, easy.

In the distance the moon hung low over the Hudson River and the New Jersey shore. But it was dark where we were, and in spite of myself I became uneasy. Parallel to us, the roar of cars raced along the highway, a drum roll before the main event, the river beyond quiescent and dark. The screech of Sidewinder's cart rankled on my nerves as he pushed, then dragged, the cart over the pebbles on the path.

We walked until we came to an underpass, and I began to have some sense of where we were. The old train tunnel, built in the mid-1800s and hidden beneath the bluffs of the park, was up ahead. Years ago the city had erected this concrete structure and buried it beneath a landscaped fill that extended Riverside Park to the water.

The Sidewinder stopped suddenly. We were standing in front of steps that led up to a wooden door. The door led into the abandoned train tunnel of the discontinued New York Central and Hudson River Railroad.

Sidewinder lifted his belongings out of the cart. I offered to help, but he shrugged me off. The moon cast a pale glow, but it was still dark where we were. I licked my lips. A heavy lock hung from a clasp on the door and the door was locked, but next to the door was a window that had lost its grate. Sidewinder slid his packages through the opening and then hoisted his body up and in and left me standing outside. He disappeared on me and then, surprise, his large head pushed through the window and his wandering eye let me know I was to follow. "Steadwell is inside?" I whispered. I don't know why I was whispering, but it seemed the thing to do.

Sidewinder vanished again and I heard the crunch of his feet on gravel. I had no choice but to follow if I wanted to find Steadwell. Heart thudding, I decided no Sidewinder would outdo me. I struggled through the narrow opening, ripping my coat and popping a button in the process. Shit. One-upmanship was for the birds. Fucking Steadwell had some explaining to do when I found him.

You can't understand the concept of pitch black until you step into it. I had stepped into pitch blackness. If I had thought it was dark outside, there was no comparison to the black inside the tunnel, entirely strange to a city boy who had never experienced utter darkness before. I couldn't see my hand in front of my face. From out of nowhere, Sidewinder grabbed my hand and pulled me after him. I yipped. Like playing blindman's bluff. I resisted his pull and tried to feel my way in front of me.

"Just follow me," he said.

I lessened my resistance and allowed him to lead me through the ghost-black tunnel. The unknown is a bitch, and wasn't that what people feared? I heard sounds, the whisper of voices, that set me on edge. We walked steadily for ten minutes. I stumbled and cussed until gradually, my eyes became accustomed to the gloom, but just barely. Sidewinder knew the terrain well, but how he managed to navigate through it was beyond me. Water dripped down from above and splashed me. I jumped.

Sidewinder said, "Water. From the melting snow."

How did he know I jumped? He could see better than I gave him credit for. I looked up at the openings overhead. Shafts of light beamed through into the tunnel, throwing a checkerboard pattern on the tunnel floor. I could see faint outlines of human forms, their bodies burrowed into crevices and alcoves and rustling nervously above. Trash sailed off a ledge and hit the ground in front of me. So many people. I was shocked. A child cried in the distance.

We moved forward, past the light into pitch-black again. Chittering noises and a sound like the muffled roar of an ocean echoed past us. Something brushed against me. In the recesses of the tunnel, eyes glowed in the dark. Wind howled down the tunnel. It was unreal and unlike anything I had ever experienced. Sidewinder shouted out greetings to people I couldn't see—the man had to be half animal—and we pressed deeper into the tunnel.

When Sidewinder finally spoke, it was an announcement. "A hundred people or so live down here on a regular basis. The crackheads, crankheads, and crazies come and go. We get along, mostly—have our own code and look out for each other. They call us mole people 'cause we live in the dark."

"Live here? What do you mean, live here?"

"English ain't your first language? What didn't you understand? We are the residents of this here tunnel."

"Are you shitting me?" And I thought Harlem was bad. "How do you survive?"

"Cut us in half, both ends wiggle."

"Ah," I said, a glimmer of understanding about this man beginning to surface.

He paused in front of a door. "Well, here we are. Home." He swung the door open and poked his head inside. "Steadwell? Got company."

We entered the concrete bunker, me trailing behind. For years I'd heard that the city's homeless lived underground, but never believed it. Well, now that I had a firsthand view, let me tell you, I was a believer.

A kerosene lamp sat in the corner and cast forms into shadows on the walls of the twelve-by-eight-foot room with a stratospherically high ceiling. Exhausted Christmas tinsel dripped down, and I wondered who could have scaled that high to decorate. No evidence of a ladder. Any minute I expected a giant to charge into the room saying Fee-Fi-Fo-Fum.

"I think this room used to be a utility room, had a refrigerator left in it. Better digs than living in the subway around Grand Central." He indicated a doorless refrigerator standing in the corner, obviously a source of pride.

I nodded, blown away by everything I'd seen, but especially at the inert form stretched out on a mattress in the center of the room. On top of the mattress lay the missing Steadwell, snoring heavily, wrapped in tattered chenille bedding and blankets. Sidewinder shook him vigorously and Steadwell, wild-eyed and confused, pulled himself awake and sat up. When he saw me he relaxed and scratched the stubble on his face. Steadwell looked bad, no question about it.

I took both him and the room in and shook my head in disbelief. From the looks of it, Steadwell's buddy, the Sidewinder, had lived here for a very long time. He had made a nest in this place, the accommodations fairly neat and well-ordered, if you could call this kind of living neat.

Kitchen supplies, utensils, cans of food, and boxes upon boxes of cereal were stacked in the far corner. Rice, flour, the essentials, you name it, and they were here—a jug of water, a chamberpot, a couch, two chairs—all made up home-sweet-home. A Persian rug covered most of the concrete floor. I was speechless. Steadwell broke the silence.

"They out to get me, man."

I swung my head in Steadwell's direction. None of this was real. "Who's out to get you?"

"They're going to wax me."

"Who, Steadwell?"

"Damned if I know. Somebody shot at me through my own damned window. They after me."

I could see he was terrified.

I put a hand on his thin shoulder and felt bone. "Why did you risk showing up to Harry's funeral?"

"To talk to Basil. Me and Harry had been pretty tight. I figured Basil would help a brother out, but I couldn't even get next to him. I got nervous, so I left."

"What aren't you telling me?"

Steadwell dropped his head. His hands shook and so did his body. Sidewinder muttered in disgust and shuffled over to the stove. While Steadwell struggled to spit out what was bothering him, Sidewinder balled up newspapers and stuffed the balls beneath the grate, added some twigs, struck a match, and lit a fire.

Then he pulled out a can opener from a drawer and attacked a can of cat food with it. Caught up with Sidewinder's actions, I couldn't pay attention to what Steadwell was saying. I said to the Sidewider, "You're not planning to eat that, are you?"

The pop of the tin brought two cats from their hiding place and they sidled over. I breathed a sigh of relief.

"Me, I ain't materialistic like Steadwell, but I live good. Don't need money. Got all I want. Steadwell over there worrying about money for retirement. Retirement, hell."

My stomach flopped, not once, but twice. I said carefully, "Steadwell, what is he talking about?"

Steadwell looked down at the floor. Sidewinder yipped, "Tell him," as he tapped the can of cat food on the edge of the kitty's dish. "Money ain't going to do you no good, dead."

Steadwell shot an angry look at his partner.

Sidewinder poured water into a coffeepot, doled out a couple of tablespoons of coffee, and set the pot to percolate on top of the makeshift stove, a wire grate set above a crown of bricks.

Steadwell said, "Fuck you, Sidewinder—when you was young, you wasn't about nothing but take, take, take. We boosted *together*, remember? You was a walking advertisement for the material life. The threads you wore, the rings and things, stereos, cars."

"Left that life twenty years ago, nigger—you still caught up in it. I got peace of mind. What you got? I got quiet. Notice how quiet it is down here?"

He paused and we all listened to the quiet.

Then he said, "A man can think down here—and live rent free, too. Been here fifteen years. What people throw out gives me everything I need. Recycle cans when I need money. Come and go as I please."

He looked over to me. "This is the good life, this is paradise, and Steadwell don't know it."

Then the Sidewinder straightened, "Tell him about the diamonds, Steadwell."

Steadwell glowered at his partner. "You call yourself a friend? The fool is daft as a loon. I don't know what he's talking about. He's living down here 'cause the V.A. wanted to lock his butt up—'cause he's crazy. They know you crazy, I know you crazy, you the only one living don't know you're crazy. Who helped your ass out every time you needed something? This is how you pay back a friend?"

Sidewinder turned to me and confided, "Your wife, baby die on you, a man gets crazy—can't help it, but I ain't never had to run from my own shadow, tell you that." And he threw a look back to Steadwell.

The Sidewinder didn't sound crazy, but he couldn't be all there, living like this. I turned to Steadwell. "Talking about how you pay back a friend, huh, Steadwell? Listen, somebody shot at me, so you'd better tell me about the diamonds."

Steadwell moaned. "They shot at you 'cause they think you know something."

"That'd be my guess."

Steadwell moaned again and hefted a butt cheek off the bed and scratched. I waited.

"My retirement's gone," he blurted, and didn't I see a tear threaten to spill down his face? I'd had enough.

"What the crap you talking about, Steadwell? It ain't like you worked for the post office or nothing. What do you mean, *retirement*?"

Steadwell whispered, as if he couldn't bear to hear the words aloud. "Diamonds was sewn up in those coats. Lots of 'em—diamonds and jewels. I found them by accident. Right after I had talked to Dap Jones about him fencing the coats to contacts outside of Harlem. I should have known better than to trust him. I called him back and told him to hold up on the deal. It would take time to remove the stones without messing up the coats. And then the asshole double-crossed me and swiped the coats, diamonds and all. Shit, I'd be in Costa Rica today, living like a king in the sun, if it hadn't of been for Dap. I'm bone tired, Amos. Bone tired. Do you understand how tired that is? Been working all my damn life. You know you can't get social security when you ain't never held a regular job."

"I know."

"And that son of a bitch fucked up everything. I should have killed him—I should have, but somebody beat me to it."

Steadwell pushed himself off the bed and recovered a coin purse from under the mattress. "This is all I got left. The rest of the jewelry I sewed back up in one of the coats. I thought it'd be safer that way." He unsnapped the purse and tumbled the contents into his hand and held it next to the gas lamp for me to take a look at.

In his palm he held two loose diamonds and a gold-and-diamond pendant. Refracted light shot around the bunker like a mirror ball exploding. And so did my brain. No doubt about it. Bet a dollar to a doughnut this was from the spoils of the recent jewel robbery.

Chapter 22

I held my head in my hands and couldn't utter a word. Steadwell didn't get it, not really. Worried about his retirement, he was jeopardizing his life. I settled back in Sidewinder's overstuffed chair—which didn't smell too bad, and was, in fact, pretty comfortable—and tried to put the pieces together.

I couldn't begin to imagine how the Sidewinder got this chair through that rabbit hole. Or indeed, how he had transported all of this stuff in here. But I had enough on my mind without worrying about the wheres and the hows of Sidewinder's furnishings. "You holding newspapers from a couple of weeks ago down here?" I asked him.

Puzzled by my request, he nonetheless rescued a couple and handed them to me. I skimmed their front pages for news about the jewel robbery and searched for the name of the store. Bingo. Not only did I find out the name of the store but I found out where it was located, on Park Avenue.

"Steadwell, Katz Furs is located where?"

"Park Avenue, near 45th Street."

"Uh-huh. Next to King Solomon's Jewelry Store?" I handed him the newspaper.

After a minute he said, "Maybe."

"You didn't put this together before?" I asked. Steadwell didn't answer. "Do you know if you ever saw anything in the paper about Katz Furs being robbed?"

"I get my news off the television. Huntley and Brinkley ain't said nothing about it," Steadwell said.

"Who tipped you off about the furs?"

"Guy who worked security for the store. Saw these coats put aside in the back of the shop. Wink-wink. Manager said they had imperfections and let my man know he wouldn't mind if they were *stolen*. So we did him a favor and stole them. Katz gets the insurance money, we get the coats, everybody's happy—until Dap messes up."

A deep furrow ran along my brow. "Where can I find this security dude?"

Steadwell shrugged. "When I got arrested, Dip Stick took off for his mama's place in North Carolina."

"Dip Stick? That's his name? And you don't know how to get in touch with him?"

Sidewinder interrupted. "Coffee, anyone?"

I nodded, "Cream, two sugars."

"We forgot to milk the cow today. You want that black?"

For a moment I had forgotten where I was. I murmured, "That'd be fine," and turned my attention back to Steadwell.

"You ever meet this Katz?"

"Why should I?"

Why indeed. "Who do you think is after you—after *us*, I mean?"

"The Somebody who stole the diamonds?"

"And who's got the coats?"

Steadwell reflected for a minute. "The Somebody who stole the diamonds?"

"Steadwell, you know the streets. This job fell in your lap. Didn't it ever seem too good to be true?"

"That's when they legit. When the job's too good to be true. I profit from people's stupidity and their greed. Somebody was stupid and they sure enough greedy, so I say, okay, this job is mine."

"You say you put the jewelry back in the lining of one of the fur coats? Only one?"

Steadwell nodded.

"Which coat?"

Steadwell looked perplexed. "I don't know—a dark one. They all look alike."

"Hell, that's what they say about us, Steadwell, not fur coats. Think."

Steadwell pouted. "It was a dark coat—hung to the floor, that's all I know."

Sidewinder handed us our coffee—French roasted it was—and we all sat and reflected for a minute, deep in our own thoughts. Patty's pawn ticket burned a hole in my pocket.

Finally, I set down my cup and said, "Well, you got a hearing on Tuesday, Steadwell. You have to show up."

"I ain't going."

"The hell you say."

"I ain't going."

"One hundred thousand in bail money says you'll be there. You can stay in one of my brownstones—I'll look out for you."

Steadwell hunched over his cup and sat silent.

"He's safer here," the Sidewinder said.

"Planning to live out his retirement? No disrespect, Sidewinder, but it doesn't seem to be Steadwell's style." Then I relented and turned back to Steadwell, "All right, look, man—stay down here until Tuesday—let me check out something. I'll pick you up early Tuesday morning, we go straight to court, I'll drop you back here."

"How'll I know you ain't being followed?"

I thought a minute. "Don't worry, old man, I'll be careful."

"It ain't careful I'm worried about, it's getting killed—that's what I'm worried about."

"You're going to die of old age, not from some bullet through your brain. Don't worry, I'll handle it." I rose to go. "Eight-thirty A.M. Tuesday. I'll bring you some clothes." I jingled his door keys in front of him. "Anyway, Steadwell, I'll be more careful than you."

Steadwell had the decency to blush.

Fatigue had set in and I was ready to go. It had gotten colder in the bunker, and Sidewinder put a small log in the grate and said he'd lead me back out the tunnel. "FYI—" he said.

"FYI what?"

"It's 11,742 steps from the bunker to where we came in—give or take a few."

I stared. "I'm sure I won't need that information."

Sidewinder's eye rolled sideways. "Um-huh. Full of yourself, aren't you? It's 11,742."

No, this man wasn't crazy at all. Not caring to engage in an eyeball-rolling contest, I repeated, "Okay, got it, 11,742 steps."

On the way out of the tunnel, in spite of myself, I counted steps and lost track at about 600.

Up on the street I counted myself lucky I had a home to go to and, by the way, a pawn ticket that needed tending. I looked around at the nearly deserted street and couldn't shake a feeling of uneasiness and some paranoia. I blamed the tunnel as I headed back to my car, glancing over my shoulder every now and then at slipping shadows around me.

Chapter 23

The experience in the tunnel stayed with me. Floating shapes and whispers filtered into my dreams. Sunday morning I lay in my bed in that twilight space between asleep and dreaming, my body not ready to come fully awake, the church bells of Harlem resounding in my head.

Shoulders and back straining, I held on to a length of cable rope and pulled with all my might, determined to bring an off-screen vision into view, but the harder I pulled, the more the picture got away from me until finally it eluded me altogether. I couldn't let it get away. I gave it one last tug, the cable snapped, and my body flew backward through the air.

Flying high through the clouds, I landed soft as cotton in a grassy meadow and I sobbed, so happy was I to have finally let go of that damn rope. But the guilt overwhelmed. Why did I feel so guilty? *God, what did I need to do?* I said, and then my eyes snapped open.

Groggy, I looked around the room. No one there. Who was I expecting? Santa Claus? I threw off the covers and my feet hit the floor. The perfect start of a perfect day. A cup of coffee and my heart would sing. I put on a pot of coffee, showered quickly, and laid out a "to do" list in my mind for the day.

Collect late rents on 128th Street. Sunday was a perfect day for it—the night crawlers slept in on Sundays. However, even as I decided on the task, I knew it was futile, yet something I had to attend to. It was me that had to keep their gas and lights going whether they paid or not. And five out of the eight apartments hadn't paid for December and it was almost January. In fact, two of the apartments hadn't paid in over nine months, or so the former owner said. Time to roust the deadbeats. It costs to gulp air on this planet and everybody has to pay, one way or another. I tucked in my shirt and buckled my belt.

If I didn't keep on them, they never would pay. January I'd be serving up notices to vacate. That Honduran drug dealer was leaving, that was for sure. One thing people couldn't get about Harlem—this community was as ethnically diverse as all of New York, a melting pot inside a melting pot. Difference being, mostly black people lived here. On purpose I skipped his apartment. Though I'd joined a citizens' group and documented evidence of his drug activities, including license plates and physical descriptions of his cohorts, the cops still wouldn't arrest him. To oust him for nonpayment of rent was my only recourse.

Off to work. I slipped my .25 in my pocket. Days like this I missed my numbers operation. But that business had its drawbacks, too. The possibility of jail time being one of them, and I was done with all that. At the entrance to the building, the door swung in when I touched my key to it. Somebody had messed with the locks again. I bent down to look. Looked as if somebody had beat the lock with a sledgehammer. For God's sake. What's the matter with these fools—somebody forgot their key?

Frustrated, I kicked the door. I'd have Seltzer replace the lock tomorrow. That meant new keys for everybody, one more thing to take care of.

As if I didn't have enough to do. In the entryway I looked up. Somebody had shot out the bulb again. And discarded needles on the stairs. Damn.

I started banging on apartment doors—half-drunk, tore up, didn't matter, I rousted the tenants' butts out of bed. Most of them blamed Christmas for the fact that they didn't have my rent money. Me, I couldn't understand it. If you budget Christmas along with your bills, you should have no problem. But the world doesn't think like a landlord does. *Last* is when you pay your rent. Last. After haircuts, Friday night movies, a new outfit, doctor's bills, and groceries. Last.

I used to empathize with my tenants, but four years in the business and you begin to see the big picture. For some people, not paying your rent is another form of welfare, subsidized living, and some have got the con down to a science. They subsist for a year not paying rent and the Department of Housing and the New York courts back them up. Then they go rent another place and start the process all over again.

I'm thankful that the tenants on 128th Street don't give me headaches. For the most part, with a few exceptions, they're a good bunch of people. I count them as friends—family, even. And just as I was about to bang on another door, I stopped myself. Speaking of family. Wilbur. God, with all this stuff about Steadwell, I'd forgotten him. Wilbur was definitely family. Well, I wouldn't put it off any longer—I'd talk to him today.

The last door I knocked on—after I'd pounded for five minutes—the Nigerian answered, the only one in the building that had a job. He slid the peephole open, saw it was me and opened the door, a lead pipe held down by his side. I looked at the pipe and he set it down, but his embarrassed look told me he didn't have the rent.

"So sorry, Mr. Brown. Thought it was the drug dealers banging on my door. They do that, you know."

"Yes, I know. I'm sorry—I'm trying to do something about that but it's hard to get them out, if you know what I mean."

He nodded and I waited. "I've come for the rent." He looked back over his shoulder as if he expected the rent to come flying from back there. When it didn't, he turned back to me and said, "My wife is sleeping. She doesn't know. I was laid off this month—before Christmas. I will find a new job soon, I am looking. If you could, please take this—" He reached in his pocket and pulled out a few bills.

I looked at the bills and looked back at him. Without another word, I stuffed them in my pocket. His baby cried fitfully in the back room. "January's rent is due soon."

"I know, I know. My papers—it is hard. I am doing what I can. I am not afraid to work, you know."

"I know you're not. You'll find something soon. Good luck, Mr. Bosompin." I turned and left. What else was there to say?

You don't have to go far to find someone worse off than you. Had this been the guilt I dreamt of? The experience in the tunnel had stayed with me. What if someone like Mr. Bosompin was forced to live down in that tunnel with his wife and child? Gave new meaning to the phrase every day above ground is a good day. My thoughts moved on to Wilbur and that was really painful. Wilbur was one of the good guys.

I rapped softly on Wilbur's door. After a few minutes the door opened, and Wilbur, clad in fuzzy-wuzzies and a thick robe, looked inquiringly at me. Standing slack-jawed, I was unable to utter a "hello."

He didn't look well. His skin sagged and his eyes were hollow and dark. I stared and he stared back.

"You know, don't you?" he said finally.

"Yeah."

"Come in." He turned from the door, went back into the room, and slumped into a chair, his eyes not meeting mine. Both of us couldn't find words. His hawklike face had grown even more hawk-ish. I twiddled my thumbs and he coughed. Pretty soon the cough turned into an attack and I went to him and thumped him help-lessly on the back. Blood spilled from his mouth and dribbled down his pajama top.

He waved me off and I rushed off to get water.

"Pneumonia," he said when I returned.

"Pneumonia?"

"And everything else. One doctor calls it the gay men's cancer. Ain't that something? The gay men's cancer."

"Never heard of that."

"Neither have I."

Unexpressed emotion swirled in the air between us and settled in my throat. I cleared my throat and said, "How can I help?"

"Whatever I've got, it's racing to finish me and the doctors have no clue about what to do. My immune system is out of whack. One doctor won't treat me, can you believe that?—Afraid he'll catch something." He leaned his head back on the armchair with a heavy sigh. "But what I'm worried about is Josie. What'll happen to her?"

"I put Patty in a room across the street—temporary. Maybe your situation will give her a reason to get off the drugs."

Another round of hacking coughs racked Wilbur's body and his body contorted and he pressed his hands against his chest. When he was at last able to take a breath, he smiled grimly and said, "How likely is that?"

"Well, we both know the odds aren't in her favor, but I'm hoping and—well, anything's possible. You getting well is a possibility."

Wilbur didn't say anything about that. He only said, "I've got to find her a home."

"Between Winnie and me, we can take care of her." But even as I said the words I was wondering how I could ever manage the responsibility, and Winnie worked the night shift at the post office.

"A real home. A permanent home."

"Now, Wilbur, don't get ahead of yourself. If the time ever does come, Josie will be taken care of—you can bet on it."

Wilbur bowed his head and his shoulders shook with a great and mighty force. Raw sounds vomited from his mouth—his pain flowed like molten steel across the room and seared me deeply, charring my soul. The air hung heavy with grief.

I popped my knuckles; there didn't seem to be anything else to do.

After a while, I got up quietly and left.

Chapter 24

Somebody was following me on my way to Ralphie's, I was sure of it. They were not phantoms from the tunnel either. Phantoms don't drive black Lincoln Continentals. I drove for fifteen minutes, swung by a bar on Amsterdam, parked, went in the front door and came out the back, then trotted over to a subway station on Broadway. How to burgle an apartment? I wondered if there was a manual somewhere.

Outside the apartment once again and under the shadow of a canopy of a building located catercorner to Evinrude's I watched a different doorman come and go. Charged, lightning bolts shooting up and down my spine and acting like I had just coked up, I fielded the stares of passersby with rigid smiles and quick glances at my watch as I made a pretense of waiting for someone.

I waited until a mother and two young children emerged from a taxi and the doorman hurried to assist them. One child flailed in the mother's arms and screamed bloody murder while her oldest child ran in dizzy circles around her. Packages and an unruly stroller tumbled out of the taxi. The doorman balanced packages with a prestidigitator's skill and followed the mother and her brood into the building.

I dashed across the street, stepped into the entryway, peeked around the corner—no one looking in my direction—and cantered to the door labeled STAIRS and pushed. Locked out. Shit. Out of sight of the menagerie, I was also out of luck—unless . . . Three keys dripped from the key ring. I played eeny-meeny, excluded a key that was obviously a car key and stuck another key into the door—it clicked. Success.

An old man entered the lobby just as I slipped through the door. My heart was pumping. Did he see me? I clutched my chest. This kind of activity was injurious to one's health. There'd be no question I didn't belong in the building. I was black, after all, and hadn't yet seen one black person set foot inside. Let's hope the old man was blind in one eye and couldn't see out the other.

I took the steps two at a time. By the time I reached the fourth floor, I was ready for pulmonary resuscitation, and that door was locked. Didn't the building have fire codes and who was following them? In case of fire—die, motherfucker?

The key worked again, and I stepped into a lushly carpeted hallway. Noiseless, I walked down the hallway, located Evinrude's apartment, used the key, and slipped inside and tripped over an upright vaccuum cleaner standing just inside the door.

Palms sweaty, I grabbed the machine before it toppled and halted at the doorway. A sound came from the kitchen. Footsteps approached. I looked wildly around and jumped into a hall closet and crammed myself into the small space.

"Hello," someone said. "Mr. Evinrude?" The feet padded past me. The front door opened, then closed and the feet padded back to the kitchen. The maid. I cracked open the closet door and hesitated, listening to the tinkling of dishes. Just as I was about to run for the front door, the kitchen noise stopped suddenly and footsteps padded back to the foyer. I closed the closet door and wrapped coats around me. Some disguise. I hoped she wasn't headed for the closet. The maid turned the light on and I sweated. The vacuum cleaner started up and droned on for fifteen minutes. My right leg began to numb. Damn, how dirty could the carpet be?

The machine stopped finally. There was a bump against the closet door and the handle turned. I grabbed it and held fast. A tug of war began. Ha-ha, I won, but sweat dripped from my armpits.

I heard a fusillade of Spanish and then she kicked the closet door in a fit of anger. Minutes went by, the lights went off. Then the front door opened, closed, and locked. I waited another minute, and coast clear, came out of the closet and wouldn't Wilbur get a chuckle out of me saying that.

I tripped over the fucking vacuum cleaner again. Damn. Electricity shot up my sleeping leg. When I was finally able to stand, I hobbled through a quick tour of the room and headed for the place where secrets lay—the bedroom.

I found no coats, no jewelry, no nothing—well, nothing but an interesting collection of sex toys that set my mind to thinking. The place was pretty bare, no sense that it was home for someone. I went back through the apartment, searching more carefully this time, in drawers and cabinets and behind pictures. Nothing. Did I think answers would magically fall in my lap? That this was going to be easy?

Convinced that this search had yielded no results, I did my best to leave the place as I found it. Before I left I put the vacuum cleaner away. Seemed like the right thing to do. And what do you know. On the shelf in the closet sat a cash box. Locked. I picked it up and shook it and then carefully replaced it. Well, when I met Ralphie on Tuesday, I'd be one step ahead of him.

Chapter 25

Monday I thought I'd take a break from it all, but that didn't happen. Instead I drove to Pennsylvania and checked Patty into rehab at a small facility nestled among rolling hills, not far from a little burg called Oneonta, which, in turn, was not that far from the Catskills. The rehab site was known for the effectiveness of its treatment program. There Patty might stand a chance. New York City's drug rehabilitation treatment centers and hospitals were overcrowded and just not doing the job. Addicts were recycled like tin cans.

When Miss Ellie called me with the news that Patty was in a bad way, I went directly across the street and laid the decision in Patty's lap. I brought it to her, and Patty came through. She told me what she had to do and why. Sometimes you need a reason for things. A reason your heart gives you.

On the way toward Oneonta the Lincoln had followed us. What struck me was the boldness of the car following. Disturbing. They didn't try to be tricky about it. I don't know whether Patty noticed the car; she never said and I kept quiet about it. She was under enough stress.

The Lincoln's driver hadn't prepared for a sightseeing trip though, and had to stop for gas. As soon as that happened, I floored Sugar and we sidetracked to the off-roads and lost them.

Now I was churning down I-87 on the return trip, and Sugar's engine hummed with delight as mile after monotonous mile sped by. Gave me some think time. Time sorely needed. I unwound and the tension in my neck and shoulders dissipated; the knots gradually released. I wondered if that's what I needed. To live life in a small town. Coming through Oneonta, people actually looked like they were happy. They smiled at each other like they did. Some of them even smiled at me.

And then I considered. Hell, but hadn't I had good times in Harlem? And would I really want to cut myself off from its life blood? I thrived, like so many others, in the hub of all its activity, complexities, and problems. A lot of famous people came out of Harlem and why? Harlem shaped you, honed you, made you strong, threw the kitchen sink at you, and made you catch that sucker and hug it to your chest with all your might. I'd said if before. My bitch, this Harlem—yes, it was.

A smile shaped itself on my lips and I felt buoyant as the lights of the city beckoned me home. I paid the toll, even paid for the car behind me, and crossed into the city.

At the house I pulled off my clothes and sipped a glass of milk before I listened to my messages. I skipped past five of them and stopped when the jazzman's voice came on. Sweets, letting me know the Italian was sitting in a booth at Wells with a friend. I checked the time; he had just called. The next message I didn't skip over either. Urgent, she said. I had to see her, she said. I deliberated and decided the second voice could wait. I had a feeling.

No time for delay, I threw on my clothes again and headed to Wells.

Wells had lost the chic, the glitter, the glam, but folks still liked to hang out there late nights for jazz, fried chicken, and waffles. I noticed the Italian right away, black hair slung down over one-half of his face—sitting with a giant friend with warts on his nose, hunched over in conversation. I eased up to their table, smiled, and lowered myself into a seat. From under the table I heard the click of a revolver. Warthog had a gun aimed at my crotch. Friendly types, they were.

"No trouble, gents," I said. "Name's Amos Brown. Trying to find out the low-down on Dap Jones. You heard of him?"

They were silent for a minute, and hooded eyes stared shrewdly, then Sergio spoke, and the language wasn't Italian.

"Shto etot yebanniy chernomaziy khochet ot nas?"

"Uspokoysa, ni stoit yevo mochit zdes."

Somewhere in the conversation I was sure he called me a nigger. Gross tattoos peeked out of his shirt, and embroidered his neck, chest, and forearms, and his partner had a few as well. Hell, they were black with tattoos—more nigger than me. I wasn't getting a good feeling. They spoke more gibberish, in a language I couldn't identify.

Then Sergio finally spoke to me, "He's dead. Haven't you heard?"

"You did business with him?"

Warthog said, "Sergei, tell him to get the fuck out of here unless he wants his balls fried up and served along with the chicken." He thumped his fist on the table for emphasis, his hand as big as a plate.

Just the size to do it, too. Sergei, huh? So the dude was Russian. Sweets had gotten both the name and nationality wrong. I looked back at the bandstand; Sweets was wailing on his sax. Italian, Russian—no difference to him.

"Easy, partner, just trying to help out someone who's been accused of Dap's murder. Know anybody have a reason to waste Dap? His enemies? You and him were into more than prostitution, right? Way I figure it, somebody killed Dap—that same somebody might be looking to kill you."

Sergei smiled at the suggestion, as if that couldn't happen in a million years and he clapped his friend on the back. "Aww, Kuchkin, he's just helping out a friend—leave him alone."

Koochie growled and didn't say anything else. Sergei turned back to me. "I knew him slightly. He knew about jazz. We'd talk. That's all. I know nothing about his business, other than he ran a few prostitutes. Sorry, I can't help you. What did you say your name was?"

"Brown. Amos Brown."

"Amos Brown." The way he savored it I knew he wouldn't be forgetting it soon. "Right. Listen, Mr. Brown, there is no problem to taking care of myself, understand?"

Did I understand? I didn't need a road map—these were heavy-duty thugs who had done hard time; *prison* written all over their faces. You could tell from the way they held themselves, the look in their eyes, and the fact that one of them held a gun on me under the table gave me a big clue. Could they have killed Dap? That was the question. From the look of things, they weren't going to help me with answers.

I got up. "Well, if you hear something—you'll let me know? For Dap's sake?"

Sergei raised his glass. "For Dap's sake? Sure, fella—I'll let you know."

I dipped my hat at them, waved to Sweets still playing on the bandstand, and got my ass out of there. Had I just come face to face with Dap's killers?

I knew before she even opened the door that I had made a wrong move. Charlize was in tears and little else. Her tits kept popping out of the robe she wore. In a fury, she stamped around her living room, boobs swinging, ranting about how Prince had done her wrong and how she was going to get revenge. She shouted *bitch* so much, I thought the word was permanently implanted in her mouth. Then she broke down altogether and I patted her shoulder. An inadequate move. Hysterical women frightened me. I waited until her tears subsided.

"Amos, what am I going to do?" she wailed.

"About what, Charlize?"

The look she gave me would have melted wax. "About Prince. It was me that pulled together enough money to start his campaign, and he throws me over for that bitch. *That bitch!*"

The bitch she was talking about was the woman I loved, so this was not an easy thing to hear. And then Charlize threw herself into my arms and sobbed on my shoulder. I stroked her lightly and she quieted.

Then she started stroking me back, softly at first and then with a little more gusto, breathing heavily and grinding her body into mine. When she turned her face up to mine it was automatic—I kissed her—and what did I do that for? Her lips consumed me, and little by little I began to drown. *Help me, help me, the rabbit said, 'fore I fall down and bust my head.*

My hands roamed over her body and I buried my head in the pillow softness of her chest and swirled my tongue around her dark nipples. We dry-humped each other and I almost cried; it had been a long time. Her body jumped and twitched and she clawed at my clothes and shed them from my body and yeah, buddy, I let her. When she started bobbing for apples—that destroyed me. I closed my eyes and lay back on her flowered couch, helpless as a child. Then she climbed on top of me, and there was no other word for it—she attacked.

I thrust myself into her and we had a ride like no other. Yee-haw. We were on the couch, we fell to the floor, she pinned me to a chair, I pounded her against a wall. Finally, our bodies untangled and we fell apart, exhausted. The perfect lover, I fell asleep immediately. No touching, no cuddling, no hugging. She woke me at midnight, and what do you know—we did it all over again.

But Charlize never answered my questions about Dap.

Two in the morning, I fondled the label on the fur coat hanging in her closet and then I crawled away from her place like a big, black spider that was really, really tired. I was spent, sore, but undeniably sated.

Ever have a sex hangover?

Last night I had made a big mistake, but I crowded those recriminations to a holding cell in my brain where it found refuge among lots of others. I chose not to deal with thoughts of the night before; I had too much to do. I got up bright and early, got in my car and took a dizzy route to Steadwell's apartment—on the lookout, but not seeing the Lincoln—the hour probably too early.

I picked up a suit, shirt and underwear for Steadwell and headed to Riverside Park. Again, I made sure I wasn't tailed. I found the door to the tunnel and the grate with no problem, slipped through it, and counted my way to Sidewinder's domicile.

In the daytime the tunnel was even more incredible. Darkness shrouded the interior but the inky blackness had lifted because of openings from the plaza level of the park through which daylight trickled. Large murals decorated the walls in the train tunnel, like cave drawings of an ancient civilization. Someone had made a great artistic effort here, no slipshod work. The quality of the graffiti amazed me. I had missed all this in the night.

And the people. Some residents, like Sidewinder, had scored actual living quarters and entrenched themselves in enclosed bunkers. Others stayed in makeshift lean-tos constructed next to the tracks, while others nested up on the ledges high above. How did people even climb up there? I tracked through trash and things I didn't want to know about, yet I found the tunnel not as dirty as it could have been, evidence that the inhabitants down here had made attempts at keeping their areas clean.

A child, about eight or nine years old, skipped by, comfortable among the denizens of the dark, and flashed me a smile. Okay, that got to me. Had he a mother or a father down here? Did he go to school?

Hanging down like stalactites were chandeliers of ice, caught in frozen suspension in the overhead grates. Unreal, I thought. Down and dirty. Another world down here. Another New York City.

No one bothered me, but I kept myself alert to any sudden movements. In the distance I saw a light flashing. Sidewinder signaling me? I followed it and it led me to Sidewinder's bunker. I didn't even blink when I recognized the light as the one cops used on tops of their radio cars.

Inside the bunker, Steadwell appeared morose but he changed into the suit I had brought for him. This was tough on him. Sidewinder escorted us to another way out of the tunnel with less wear and tear on the clothes as we pulled ourselves up and out of the tunnel through a wider opening near 79th Street.

We climbed stairs adjacent to the highway's underpass, reached plaza level, and walked uptown to where Sugar was parked. A sudden screeching of brakes coming from behind made us turn. I grabbed hold of Steadwell's coat, pulling him after me, and started to run, but two cars charged us at high speed and end-ran us, one car jumping the curb.

Doors flew open and four thugs jumped us and began beating the shit out of us. People near us scattered and ran like hell. The people across the street looked on in shocked disbelief.

A brute nearly seven feet tall dragged Steadwell, kicking and screaming, to a car. Tattooed fists rained down on me and I saw shooting stars—no chance in hell to defend myself.

What I remembered next was sky and satin blonde hair falling in my face, and a pretty white woman, with a pretty white handkerchief, pressing it against the side of my bleeding head. I thought sure I had died and an angel fluttered over me. Her harsh Bronx accent destroyed the seraphim illusion, but in my condition, beggars couldn't be choosers.

"You all right, mister?" she said.

"Where am I?" New Yorkers stepped over me or walked around. From where I lay it was an amazing sight—legs, legs, and more legs.

"I saw what happened. You want to call the police?"

Did I want to call the police? In a haze I really considered that question. *Did I want to call the police?*

I nodded my head; nausea gripped me, and it took tremendous willpower not to throw up in the pretty lady's lap.

"Here, let me help you up."

A Suit walked by, and stopped to help the lady help me. I rocked a little on my heels as they lifted me, but I managed to stand alone.

"I live three buildings down," she said. "You can make the call from my apartment."

An alarm went off. Probably one of those liberal white chicks who made causes out of black men, just my luck. The turquoise beaded necklace and the Indian bangles clinched my impression. No, she couldn't have my body. *Did I want to go to her apartment?* I think I did.

The Suit surreptitiously wiped his hands and rushed off, almost running, and I followed Blondie to her apartment, my mind beginning to buzz with the enormity of what had happened. Shit, they got Steadwell. I could have sworn I hadn't been tailed. Steadwell warned me and I didn't listen. They were more cunning than I thought.

I didn't see faces, but I knew it had been Sergei and his boys that had jumped us. What the fuck was going on? How to get in touch with Prince? Should I call the police? I had no choice—Steadwell had been kidnapped.

The hippy-dippy blonde made tea, and I cleaned my face, dusted myself off, and used her phone. She sat in the corner, a teacup poised on her lap, and listened.

I called the station house and asked for Bundt. Miracle of miracles, I was put through. The strange thing? He didn't cut me down when I related my story, but told me to bring my ass over to the 28th. When I hung up the phone, Blondie said, "You were supposed to be in court?"

I nodded. She said, "Better let me make a phone call. Superior Court, what Part?" I told her, and, smooth as silk, she picked up the phone, introduced herself as an assistant federal prosecutor, and got in touch with whomever. See, you can't always rely on first impressions. They'll steer you wrong every time. My mouth sort of dropped open, and she introduced herself officially.

"Courtney Caldwell."

"Amos Brown."

"I heard."

"So did I. Uh, thanks. Brave of you to come to my aid and invite me in."

She shrugged. "I'm an officer of the court. I see it as a duty."

"Of course," I said, and got up to go.

"You want to tell me what's going on? Maybe I can help."

"Uh, I don't think so. As you said, you're an officer of the court. Under the circumstances, might not be a wise thing to do."

She shrugged. "Whatever you say. Are you all right? You got beaten up pretty badly. You want me to call an ambulance?"

"No, skip that. Better hustle over to see Captain Bundt. You know him?"

She shook her head. "No, but I've heard of him. He has a good reputation."

I pulled on my coat. She dug in her purse and handed me her card. "Keep it, in case. You might need help down the line."

I pursed my lips. "Miss Courtney, you've razed a stereotype. From this day forward, I'll think better of white women."

She drew a bead on me. "Better? Well, I haven't been robbed, beaten or raped in the last hour, so maybe I'll think the same about black men."

I gave her a grudging smile. "Touché," I said. Feisty little number. I tipped my hat at her and left, before I really got in trouble.

Chapter 26

The temperature in Bundt's office was set to boiling. I tugged at my shirt to peel it off my body. Was this on purpose? Grilling me like the old-time hoodlums? Whatever. Bundt seemed really interested in what I had to say. And when I described Sergei he almost creamed in his pants.

"Damn Jew bastards."

Well, Bundt had a German name, but a Jew-hater? That surprised me. I gave him a puzzled look; he colored and explained himself.

"They're coming out of Russia, straight from Russian prisons. Vicious, cutthroat types. Dumped on U.S. shores, and we're in a hell of a mess. Mafiya, they're called, the Russian version of the mob. Got a stronghold out in Brighton Beach." Bundt slammed his hands on his chair, got up and paced around his small office. Mesmerized by what he said, I took it all in.

"The police department's hands have been tied in knots by the Anti-Defamation League—they're a powerful force in this city. Everybody's tiptoeing through the tulips, nobody wants to make waves. They're making a mistake on this. It ain't like these crumb-bums *practice* their religion.

Hell, way I see it, a criminal is a fucking criminal is a fucking criminal. I don't discriminate. Their Russian asses need to be locked up and the key thrown away and buried someplace. But no one wants to commit political hari-kari, and the Mafiya is getting away with murder—literally. Extortion, protection, prostitution, stolen art. Doesn't surprise me they're involved. But Harlem? They're on my turf now."

And that's what really bothered him. It bothered me, too.

Then Bundt licked his lips. "It's a hot potato issue. I've got to tread lightly."

I inserted my two cents. "And the Italians are taking this?"

"*The Italians*? The fucking Italians are making alliances with them. *Alliances*. Can you believe it?"

Then Bundt's eyes shifted away. "Hate to tell you this, but I'm not holding out much hope for your friend's survival. When I said they're vicious, Brown, I meant it. The Italians won't mess with each other's families, some sort of honor code, but these fellows will kill their *own* and not blink an eye. If your friend is with them, he's in deep trouble, that's all I got to say. They specialize in torture. How'd your friend every get mixed up with them in the first place?"

We held eyes for an instant. I reflected on what he told me and said, "Hot potato, huh? Then, some things are better left unsaid."

Bundt said, "If there's anything you're not telling me, you'd better spill it now."

To mention the diamonds would put Steadwell in further legal jeopardy, and I had to quickly decide whether that knowledge would help Bundt find him or not. I decided it wouldn't, but a lump big as a diamond stuck in my throat.

Bundt coughed. "But if you were to find out some things, uncover some things—well, it wouldn't be my fault, know what I'm saying? I'd back you up, jail the motherfuckers. I mean, I'd have to, wouldn't I?"

Yeah, Bundt was describing my ass in a sling. I understood completely. "You'll try to find my friend, Bundt?"

"Got men on it now."

"Fine. If I come up with anything you can use, I'll let you know."

"And Brown, if you were to register for carrying a piece, I'd see to it that it went through."

"Telling me to watch my back?"

"Your back, your front, your sideways, Brown. I mean it."

"Well, thanks, Captain Bundt, you've made me feel a hell of a lot better."

"Laugh, clown, but you'd better take my advice."

On that note, I left.

Outside the police station, I contemplated what I should do next. Talk to Prince, definitely. And this Evinrude guy, I'd see him tonight. Was he hooked up to the Russian mob?

Meanwhile, it takes one to know one. I went to visit Basil.

Chapter 27

Basil's office at the pool hall was no-frills. He hadn't inherited Harry the Monkey Chaser's love of excess. African art and sculpture graced the walls and tabletops. I checked out his threads. His mustard colored gabardine suit would look good on me. Basil ushered me into a seat and announced without me saying anything, "The Mafiya is after you and you want my help."

I stared at Basil. How did he know?

"I tried to warn you about that Brighton Beach bunch, Amos, at the funeral. Couldn't get your attention."

"Basil, in this case, you should have been more insistent."

"It's not my style to push."

Murder and mayhem, he had no problem with; being pushy, he couldn't handle. Yeah, right.

"How much do you know, Basil?"

"An open-ended question."

"I have a feeling you know what I'm talking about."

Basil shrugged. "Sergei was putting the muscle to Dap, ripping off Dap's profits from prostitution. Dap was scared shitless, the spineless motherfucker—he offered Steadwell's coats for a payoff.

"Coats that weren't his," he added.

"Hey, guess what? They weren't Steadwell's, either. Amos, you're over your head. I can deal with the Russians. If worse comes to worst, I can enlist the help of the Jamaicans—they're just as treacherous as the Russians."

"In exchange for what?"

Basil smiled. "You have influence with Catherine. She's my cousin and I don't want to fight her, but I need Harry's house and she's refusing to give it up."

I didn't mention I had no present currency with Catherine. Instead I said, "Basil, for God's sake, what's a house? You've got money, you can buy a house. Why is it necessary for you to have Harry's house?"

Basil leaned forward. "There are hidden rooms, niches, and escape routes built into that house, plus several *millions* of dollars of heroin and cocaine stored in a vault in a hidden room in the basement. I want that house."

I gaped at him. "Does Catherine know about this?"

"I don't want to destroy Catherine's image of her uncle. We're family, after all. Harry has always been special to her, in spite of everything. She's a little naïve, you know."

Basil had understated. That was exactly the problem that I had with Catherine; we discussed it many times, her feelings about her uncle a source of conflict for the both of us. She was aware of what he did, yet she didn't want to *know* the depth of his criminality. Inheriting Harry's vast wealth hadn't bothered her at all. I'd have choked on the money myself, but Harry's death meant Catherine finally had a chance to catapult herself to the rank of society maven, which is what she secretly desired—the opportunity to attend teas and afternoon luncheons in the hills of Englewood, New Jersey.

Then Basil jumped up, the first time I'd seen him lose his cool. The pulse in his neck jumped. "The stupid bitch talked about litigation and bringing the cops into this. The cops? Is she crazy? She doesn't know what she's stirring up. If we can't agree, she'll have to be dealt with."

Basil had issued a real threat. Quiet settled in the room. And Bundt accused the Russians of having no heart when it came to family? "Look, Basil, it will be a hard sell to dissuade her about Harry's place."

"It will be a harder task to deliver you Steadwell and keep you from harm."

"You'll deliver Steadwell?"

"No guarantees. It may already be too late."

I blinked. He was right. "I'll talk to her."

"Right away," Basil said.

"Right away," I answered.

Besides, it was me that brought up the idea of litigation in the first place, and I was feeling guilty.

Chapter 28

Catherine had moved out of Harlem three years ago. In her mind she had moved years before. Another bone of contention between us. I roamed the space in her Queens apartment that had no view. Time was crucial. I talked, intense as a motherfucker, and she moved back and forth, packing and stacking boxes. Whatever I was saying, it wasn't getting through. The clock ticked while we talked.

"Amos, I would think you'd be happy for me, finally getting out of this cooped-up apartment into something better, a house that belongs to me."

"Catherine, the house is *purple*."

She looked at me as if I were crazy. "It can be painted."

"Basil's willing to pay good money for it."

"I don't care—it belonged to Uncle Harry, he wanted me to have it, and now it's mine."

I stared, and in the bluntest way possible I finally said, "It's a *drug house*, Catherine, built to house, store, feed, and hide criminals and their drugs. Millions of dollars worth of drugs, weaponry, and who knows what else is hidden in that house, and Basil is pissed that he can't get to it. It has secret tunnels and escape routes. Sell Basil the house or the next thing you know the Feds will be called, you'll be arrested, and there go your plans for a career of hobnobbing with the nouveau riche of Englewood."

Catherine dropped a package that she was holding. It hit her toe, which must have hurt. "Hobnob with the rich? That isn't why I want the house."

"No?"

She turned away and didn't answer the second time, but I could see she was troubled. "You say there's drugs in the house?"

I nodded.

"Are you sure?"

I bobbed my head again.

"It couldn't be as much as you said. Harry had stopped doing that."

I groaned. "Catherine, just how in hell do you think Harry came by the considerable fortune you are inheriting?"

Her eyes flashed. "Harry owned beauty shops, dry cleaners, two grocery stores—he had a lot of businesses. His lawyer explained it to me."

"He also owned an airplane that smuggled drugs and had off-shore accounts. His businesses were bought and paid for by drugs and used to launder money. What planet do you live on?" She colored, and I stood up. I didn't have time for this. Steadwell's life was at stake and Catherine here was in fucking denial.

"I think you'd better leave," she said.

"I think you'd better make a decision and make it quick. Steadwell's life is in jeopardy and so is yours."

Catherine didn't even blanch. She eyed me steadily—the woman was tough as nails. Naïve, but tough.

"What are you talking about?" she said.

I said nothing, but she got the point. She stopped packing.

"Cousin Basil thinks he can scare me?"

There didn't seem to be a right answer for that one, so I played dumb again.

"All right, Amos. You tell Basil, on one condition. I see it for my-self. Every room, every hidden tunnel. Basil has to show it to me—then I'll believe it."

"Done."

"Done."

"Get your coat."

"Now?"

"If not now, when?" I said, and breezed her out the door.

A half-hour later we picked up Basil, and in another half-hour, our two cars were parked outside the gates of King Harry's lavender mansion.

Chapter 29

It said "King Harry's Castle" over the arch at the top of the electric gate. Basil zapped the remote, the gate opened, and we followed his Mercedes up a winding driveway and parked both cars in front of the entrance to the house. At the door, Catherine handed the keys over to Basil. Stepping into the foyer, the first thing I did was look up at an enormous skylight and a ballroom-sized chandelier hanging from the ceiling.

We strode briskly through the house, each room we passed more lavish than the next. Any other time I would have grooved on the screening room with a mounted screen and luxurious red leather chairs set in two rows, each with built-in tray tables, drink holders, and ashtrays, but Steadwell was in danger and my nerves were shot. Catherine had seen all this. She was as anxious as I was to get to the basement level of the house where Basil said the illegal stash and other things were kept.

Basil wanted me to park in the living room while he revealed the house's secrets to Catherine, but she insisted I accompany her, so Basil relented. He was not happy about it, I can tell you, but he bit his tongue and led us into the dining room where Harry had a twenty-foot formal banquet table with twenty chairs set around it.

Basil stepped to a mounted china cabinet that covered a third of the wall and turned a lock beneath one of the shelves; the wall, powered by some kind of hydraulics, slid open to reveal a narrow hallway and steps leading down to the basement.

Catherine's eyes bugged as we stepped through the opening, the wall slid shut behind us, and automatic lights blinked on. Because of my height I had to stoop as we marched single file down a narrow corridor until we came to an even narrower staircase. We descended it and at the bottom, I fully expected to see Boris Karloff or one of his boys jump out, but we came face-to-face with a steel door instead.

Basil punched in a code. I noticed—4712. Couldn't help it—a habit, memorizing numbers used to be my thing. The door clicked open, and we found ourselves in a dank tunnel with a dirt floor. Catherine shivered. I took her arm. The tunnel wound ahead in front of us for about fifty yards—we walked until we reached a fork and the tunnel divided in two. In one direction the path was undisturbed and untrod upon, in the other I saw evidence of footprints. At the crossroads and contrary to the poet's suggestion, we didn't take the path less traveled. And did it make a difference?

Well, Basil said the less traveled path led to a highway five miles away. The path we were taking led us up to another steel door—the door of a vault. It took him about five minutes, but Basil finally got it open. Inside, he tugged a chain and a light came on, its blue glow casting an eerie light down on the three of us.

Catherine gasped and I gawked. Bags of uncut heroin and cocaine climbed the walls of the vault and covered most of the available floor space. Basil wasn't kidding. There was a fortune in here. On a shelf sat five metal storage boxes that Catherine opened and peeked inside, and then rifled through the contents. Money and more money, two passports for Harry under two different names, fake IDs, and other false documents filled the boxes. Nothing left to chance.

Catherine slid a box off a shelf and said, "Well, here's a donation to someone's political campaign." No one said anything, but my stomach roiled. She handed the box to me and then lifted up the second money box.

"And this one? This one is for shopping." Her look to Basil

dared him to say anything. Basil merely smiled. Just as we were turning to exit the vault, the door slammed shut. It startled Catherine and it certainly raised a small panic in me. We both looked to Basil.

He pressed a red button, we heard a whirring sound, and on our right, another door, one I hadn't noticed before, sprang open. Jesus. Smoke and mirrors and a lot of fucking doors. That Harry was one smart criminal.

We stepped out into a cool room which turned out to be a large and well-stocked wine cellar. It was dark inside, and Basil lit a kerosene lamp sitting on a shelf and held it in front of him as we followed him out of the cellar and down another corridor. We passed two rooms on the right with locks on them. "What's in there?" I said, curious.

"Bodies," Basil said.

Catherine misstepped, eyes large as saucers. Basil laughed. "Just kidding—my little joke."

Catherine regarded Basil. A joke? I couldn't be sure that Basil wasn't telling the truth.

We found the freight elevator and it took us back upstairs. When we reached the foyer where our little journey had begun, Catherine said to Basil, "Make me an offer. I'll sign the papers."

"And Steadwell?" I said to Basil.

"My boys are on it. You'll have an answer tonight."

I was distracted and Catherine was silent on the way back to her apartment. The two cash boxes lay on the seat between us, effectively making sure that ours wasn't a cozy ride. Every once in a while I sneaked a peek at her, but she stared out the window and wouldn't look in my direction. I breathed in her perfume as we crossed the Washington Bridge and merged into the Bronx Expressway, entertained by a vivid fantasy about her and me.

When we got to the Whitestone Bridge, she spoke. "You've accused me before of being a snob. You're the bigger snob, Amos Brown, and you don't even know it."

Screech. My daydream halted abruptly and it took me a moment to catch up to what she was saying. Puzzled, I said, "You're going to explain that, right?"

"I saw the look on your face when I took the money. You don't think I should take it."

I shrugged my shoulders. "Buy some dresses—you deserve it. I just don't think you should support somebody's political ambitions, especially when all they're on is a power trip."

"What are you talking about?"

"Prince. I'm talking about Prince. He wants to represent West Harlem down at city hall. With him, it ain't about representing nobody but himself."

"You think I'm going to give Prince money? Are you crazy? Or do you think I am?" Catherine laughed and I turned to look at her.

"Then who are you giving it to?" I said.

"You don't know me. You have no idea who I am, do you, Amos Brown?"

Oh, shit. This was turning into one of *those conversations*. Should've kept my trap shut. I waited. The explosion should come soon. And it did.

"See, that's what I'm talking about. You make assumptions about me and they're wrong. They're always wrong. Why do you do that? Why?"

Her outburst baffled me. "Not always wrong. Didn't I see you two get all chummy at Harry's funeral? What was that about?"

"Chummy? *Chummy*?" She was practically apoplectic now.

"Don't knock my choice of words. That's the only word I could think of without getting insulting."

She glared. "*Now* you're insulting. Because a man smiles at me, I'm going to hand him thousands of dollars?"

When she put it like that, it did sound kind of stupid.

"How desperate do you think I am? Oh, what do you care, anyway?" She flounced back in her seat and crossed her arms. A single tear began a journey down her face.

This wasn't going well. Catherine confused me. I decided to keep my mouth shut and drove in silence to her Queens apartment.

At her building, I shut off the engine and we sat in silence, her body hunched deep against the door on the passenger's side, arms still folded.

I brushed her cheek with my hand. In a low voice she at last spoke. "I always wanted—more than anything—to be respectable. Can you understand that? Having an uncle like mine made it impossible. But I tried—went to nursing school, moved out of Harlem. I loved my uncle, but was ashamed of him." Her eyes filled with tears.

Catherine with her boxing gloves off. A sight to behold. She grabbed my hand in a death grip. Lightning thrilled through my body. I drew her roughly to me and caressed her face, the cash boxes gouging me in the thigh, as I pushed my tongue deep into her mouth. Deep enough to reach her heart. At least I tried, but she pushed me back, gasping for air.

I started to ease the cash boxes out of the way, but she wanted the barricade there. She stopped me. I said, "What? You're going to let money come between us?" This strange look settled on her face. I bent toward her, inching one of the boxes to the floor. Then I nibbled at her neck, her hair. She quivered, and all at once rose up on her knees and crawled over the boxes and grabbed my shirt. She kissed me so fiercely I almost passed out. In one practiced move she straddled me and rocked her hips against me. I thrust her skirt up over her thighs. Pure confection and then I grabbed her butt and held on. We slammed against each other so hard the car started shaking. She kept bumping up against the steering wheel in rhythmic bumps. At the height of our passion, the horn blared loudly. I thought she had farted.

After that, the lovemaking stopped. Embarrassed, she scrambled back to her side of the car, banging her knees on the boxes as she went. She pulled her dress down and rubbed her knees; I straightened my shirt. We both took a time out, with heavy breathing on both sides.

Then she pushed herself out of the car, grabbed the cash boxes and said, "I want babies, Amos. I want a family. You rejected me once, I'm not letting you do it again."

I was rendered speechless. All I could say was, "I'll call you." The lyrics to a blues song flashed through my head. *If you want a do-*

right, all-night woman—you got to be a do-right, all-night man. I wasn't that by a long shot.

Her parting shot? "For your information, *I'm* the one running for an assembly seat, idiot, representing Harlem," she said.

Why did I have to be the idiot?

I laughed and said, "You live in Queens, for God's sake."

It was the laugh that did it. Her eyes flashed; she hiked the cash boxes under her arms and stalked into her building without another word. I knew that this time, she had walked out of my life for good.

Idiot.

I parked in Harlem and took the subway to 72nd Street, knowing I'd never find a place to park, and hotfooted it from the train station to Prince's office and passed the same dress shop where I had bought the red dress. I frowned. *She wanted babies.*

Prince wasn't in but Charlize was. "Has anybody been in contact with Prince? Anybody with a funny accent?" I said.

"No. Why would they?"

"Charlize, the coats. The Russian mob is after the coats. They want to know where they are. Prince is Steadwell's lawyer. They might figure he knows."

Her face turned chalk white, no small feat for a black woman. "But he doesn't. He doesn't know anything. What could they possibly want with eighteen fur coats?"

"Tell your boss to be careful. His life might be in danger. If I were you, I'd close up the office and go home."

Charlize's hands trembled and she fell apart, right in front of me. "Oh God, what have I done? Oh God—" she cried.

"What are you talking about? None of this is your fault."

"I told him to take the case. I told Prince—"

"If it was you that convinced Prince, I'd say you did a good thing. Steadwell is innocent, you know. But he got caught up in things out of his control. There's more to the story. Stuff I didn't even know about."

Charlize froze like a trapped animal and waited for me to take aim and fire.

I hesitated and then spilled it all. She had a right to know. "The jewel robbery that's been in the papers the last month?" I said.

"Yes?"

"The stones were stitched in the linings of Steadwell's stolen fur coats and the Russian Mafiya is after the loot."

A hiss like a balloon deflating escaped from Charlize's lips—her eyes widened and her head lolled. I reached out to grab her, but I missed. She fell in a dead faint to the floor, her titty slipping out of my hand.

Chapter 30

Ilaid her out on Prince's couch—let Prince deal with her. I locked the office door behind me and trotted, worried, back to the subway. If Steadwell's abductors found out that Steadwell didn't know where the missing coats were, he'd be history. Then again, if they figured he did know . . .

I pushed my hands deeper into my coat pocket. A train rumbled and signaled its approach. Bundt mentioned torture. That idea snaked around my brain and I shuddered to get rid of it.

Only one fur coat really mattered—the one holding the precious stones. But did the Russians know that? So preoccupied was I that I didn't notice the pair when they sidled up next to me. The rank odor of someone's garlic breath assailed me, and startled, I turned and looked into the dead eyes of Sergei and his freaky bodyguard.

"Jump, motherfucker," Sergei ordered, and shouldered me to the platform. I grabbed hold of a steel post and wrapped myself around it, kicking them back with one leg as hard as I could. The train screeched into the station, emitting a howl that echoed mine. Sergei yelled, *jump* again, and his seven-foot-tall sidekick tried to pry my fingers off the post.

The train bore down steadily. I clung to the post with all my might, my muscles straining. The train whooshed past, grazing my body and hurtling me into the giant. A woman screamed as our bodies entangled. We fell in a heap on the platform. Shouts rained around us, but it didn't matter to the giant. He bench pressed me over his head—the freak was not human—and in a rage flung me full-force into the side of the train. My body hit, blood spurted from my nose, and I felt as if my body had splintered into a million pieces. People exiting from the doors of the train stumbled over me. I staggered to my feet. A sharp pain in my left side wrung the breath out of me. I gasped and faltered, and clung again to the post. Were my ribs broken?

The Russians had disappeared. I looked to where they had taken off, but they were nowhere in sight.

Bent over and barely standing and nose bleeding, I caught the next train smoking. White-hot anger fueled me—no other gas left in my tank. Inside the car I leaned against the train doors, panting, and stanched the blood coming from my nose with a handkerchief. The other passengers gave me a wide berth.

Pain shot up and down my side and my entire body throbbed, but by the time I reached Evinrude's stop I was at least able to stand upright and take tentative steps. I kept walking, up the subway stairs and into the street. The more I walked, the better it was. I threw the bloody mess of a handkerchief into the nearest trash can.

At Evinrude's building my appearance raised eyebrows, but frankly, I didn't care. The grim look on my face intimidated the doorman and he phoned Evinrude and sent me on my way immediately. Anything to get rid of me.

A man of medium height, weight, and stature, wearing glasses, opened Evinrude's door. I lunged for him, grabbed him by the collar with both hands, and pushed him back into the room. Hazel tried to come between us, but I didn't plan on releasing Ralphie until he came up with some answers. *Somebody* had to give me some answers.

I said, "You got ties to the Russian mob?"

Startled, Ralphie said, "What? No—no—"

"What do you have to do with fur coats?"

"I—I sell them."

Taking him by his collar, I swung him around and slammed him against the wall. "You Katz?"

"What? No—Katz doesn't exist. Katz is dead. Goldberg owns the store. I'm the manager."

"The manager?" I yelled. "The manager that arranged for fur coats to be stolen? *That* manager?" Grimacing, I released him. This was hurting me more than it was hurting him. "All right. You've got ten seconds. Tell me, what's it all about, Ralphie?" and I smacked him.

Ralphie's glasses flew off his nose and he grabbed for them. Then he said accusingly to Hazel, "You said it was the dope man with the weed." Hazel looked struck dumb herself; she didn't know what was happening. She avoided Ralphie's eyes and eased into a chair.

"Five seconds," I shouted.

Ralphie whimpered, "Please, I don't know anything."

"I don't think that's true, Ralphie. You set up my friend. He may not live to see tomorrow because of those damn fur coats. I think it's your fault."

Ralphie looked helpless—he was almost blubbering.

"Ben, the owner, told me to arrange it. He had paid out large sums of money—for protection, he said. His life was being threatened, they wanted more. I suggested that if his furs got stolen he could collect the insurance and get them off his back."

"The diamonds?"

Ralphie's jaw dropped. "You know about them?"

"Everybody knows about them—that's the problem, Ralphie."

Ralphie clammed up. I pulled out my gun and aimed it at him. That primed the pump. Words flowed like diarrhea out of Ralphie's mouth then.

"Ben changed plans without letting me know. Russian mobsters were extorting from his brother, too."

"His brother own Solomon's Jewelry Store?"

Ralphie nodded.

"His name Solomon?"

"No. Ken."

"Ken?"

"Ken Goldberg. They're twins. Not identical—anyone can tell them apart. Anyway, Ken decided it would be better to collect on his jewelry, instead of Ben's furs. They could get more money. They'd fake a jewel robbery and collect the insurance money and pay for the protection. Ben sewed the jewelry and loose diamonds in the coats for transport to Russia."

"Why?"

"They were legally exporting the coats, but using them to smuggle the jewels into Russia."

"And why didn't we hear in the newspapers about the coats being stolen?"

Ralphie shrugged. "As I said, they weren't supposed to be stolen, and Ben didn't report it. The police and the Russians would be suspicious if there were two robberies so close to each other."

"Why to Russia? The USSR went bankrupt, last I heard."

"Ah, but the black market is very alive. The brothers could make a huge profit through Ben's KGB contacts.

Chatty Ralphie was not convincing. Something bothered me. "So why is the Mafiya after me? Why aren't they after *your* ass?"

Ralphie looked blank. "I—I don't know."

"Isn't your boss upset with you?"

"It wasn't my fault. He's my father-in-law."

I narrowed my eyes. And then I indicated Hazel.

"And where did you get her coat? Her coat come off the gonna-be-stolen rack?"

Ralphie got indignant. "No. I bought it. Bought it with my own money."

Sure he did. Hazel gave him a drippy smile, and I headed for the closet. And while he's jabbering on, I'm thinking numbers. The number nineteen, specifically. How it's an odd-ass number for stolen product. Usually things go in numbers like 15-20-25 or 2-4-6. I pulled the cash box off the shelf. Huh. Nineteen, the number of coats Steadwell stole. Nineteen, the number of coats Dap stole. No, there were twenty coats to begin with—I'd bet on it. I wasn't a numbers banker for nothing. I was good with numbers.

Ralphie's eyes got round. I used the pocketknife on my key chain and popped the lock. What do you know? A stash of jewelry and loose diamonds. "These come out of the coat you gave Hazel, Ralphie?"

While Ralphie had his epiphany, I had mine. An invisible hand slapped me upside the head. What was that Charlize had said? I never asked how her how she got her fur coat—or, more importantly, when.

I needed to see that woman—and right away.

Chapter 31

Charlize's chair lay sideways on the floor of the outer office. Scattered papers and spattered blood made patterns on the desk and carpet. The door hung drunken off its hinges. Prince sat unmoving, his eyes red-rimmed.

"They've taken her."

Useless information. Any fool could see what happened, but Prince's fear ran deep as mine, and useless conversation was all we were good for at the moment.

Prince handed over a balled-up piece of paper. I spread it open. A note from Charlize's abductors.

"They want the coats," Prince said. "This is my fault. She raised money for me—with the coats. That's why Charlize—that's why I took Steadwell's case."

My resentment of Prince evaporated in the face of this latest development. He was devastated, it was clear.

"What will they do to her?"

My hands hung at my sides—I had no words to answer him. Prince understood what they were going to do—the note said it all—after calling Charlize a whore bitch, it said Prince would find her tricking and they named the corner.

"We call the police, they'll kill her."

"I know."

"What'll we do, Amos?"

"Give them what they want."

"You know where the coats are?"

"I know where one coat is."

I didn't wait to explain—there was no time—and Prince wouldn't know what I was talking about, anyway. I tore out of the office. Prince's shouts trailed me down the hallway. I didn't wait for the elevator—I ran down four flights of stairs. I had to get to Bunky's pawnshop.

But first I'd better pick up my car and my .38.

Nobody had to tell me there was a body in front of my brownstone. The flashing lights from the cops' cars gave me a clue. The yellow tape cordoning off the entrance to my brownstone gave me another. But still I wasn't prepared for what I saw. Winnie, looking down on the scene out of an upstairs window. Wilbur, looking like death himself, sat huddled on the stoop. Captain Bundt himself paced back and forth in front of the crime scene. When he saw me coming, he motioned his men to make way for me.

"Been looking for you," he said.

People from the coroner's office were about to remove the body. They balanced the stretcher a few feet away, flesh bundled in a bag, zipped tightly up.

"You want to identify the body?"

"What's a captain doing at a crime scene?"

"I recognized the address. I thought it might be you."

I blinked rapidly and nodded. My nostrils stung. People ought not to kill one another. They really shouldn't. Christmas, joy, hope, and love, gone in a whisper. The floodgates of cruelty had opened and delivered death. I gestured toward the body. "Let's do this."

But I wasn't prepared. I wasn't prepared for the loud unzipping. I wasn't prepared for the grotesque condition of Steadwell's face. His head resembled a huge soccer ball, bloated, round, and colored purple. One eye dangled from its socket. He had cuts, scars, and blood on his face. Someone from the ME's office lifted Steadwell's arm out of the bag.

I gagged. "That's enough. It's Deacon Steadwell," I said.

"You seen this, Captain?" the man said. "You seen this?"

Steadwell's fingers had been lopped off, his hand a bloody, pulpy mess.

"What the hell you doing? Put that back," Bundt growled.

Even Bundt turned away from the body. It was a sight, let me tell you. Then I noticed Wilbur shivering on the steps. I said to Bundt, "You need him?"

Bundt looked over at Wilbur. "No, not any more. He found the body."

"Let him go inside, then."

Bundt shrugged. "No problem."

I walked over to Wilbur, helped him up—his bones felt like twigs—and I ordered him inside.

He looked into my eyes—he knew what I was feeling—and said, "You need something, let me know, Mr. B." When Wilbur said that—no shit—that's when I broke down.

For a man who never had a real family, to watch people close to me leave me, in the most unnecessary way, ripped the heart and soul from me, fragment by fragment. Powerful feelings churned inside me. I wanted someone dead. I wanted to do to them what they had done to poor Steadwell. Bundt knew that. He saw my eyes.

I gave one of his detectives a description of the two Russians. Bundt cautioned, "Don't do it. Let us take care of it."

It's hard to kill someone—especially up close, face to face. You see the human things about them, imperfections, a vein throbbing in their head, a stubble of beard—human things that connect them to you and you to them and it's hard, really hard. But rage had me in its grip, and I trembled from its force. I was ready to do most anything.

Bunky's Pawn Shop was sealed tight as a drum, iron bars protecting it from a rapacious public. I leaned on his bell; Bunky lived in an apartment above his shop. No answer. What did I expect? It was one in the morning, and all the shops along this stretch of street were closed, except for a liquor store that stayed busy with customers, and a bodega three doors down from which a child emerged carrying a loaf of white bread—who needed white bread at one in the morning?

To storm Bunky's had been a bad idea. And only a one in twenty chance I would be right. My gambler's soul didn't like the odds, but there was no help for it. I looked at the sign on Bunky's window. The shop would be closed early tomorrow—New Year's Eve. New Year's? Already? Where had the time gone?

I tried five pay phones, but their guts had been destroyed or were not working, so I invaded Prince's crib, pulled him out of bed, and made him bring Charlize's key along to open her apartment. We desecrated Charlize's fish tank and plucked out stones and gravel that lined the bottom of the tank and began sewing them into the lining of Charlize's mink coat. Then I called Basil.

Three o'clock in the morning my car was parked down the block from the hooker's corner. Sergei leaned, one foot against a building that had a HOTEL sign out front, smoking a cigarette and watching the women ply their trade. The giant wasn't around and that made me nervous; my eyes constantly surveying the street. One of the women wore a frothy blond wig and had on some sort of tiger-striped miniskirt. She turned in our direction, hesitated for a second, then broke away from the others and started walking toward my car, swinging her hips.

Beyond her, a man scurried out of the hotel, followed by a girl who looked to be in her teens. She adjusted her clothes and handed money over to Sergei. So Sergei had taken over Dap's stable. Sitting next to me, Prince groaned. Sweat popped out on his freckled nose, and he said of the woman approaching, "What is she doing? What is that woman doing?" I knew it had been a bad idea to bring him, but he had insisted.

She rapped on the car window. I kept my eyes on Sergei and the street. Sergei noticed us, probably recognized the car. Shit.

"Hey, remember me?" Tiger-skirt hollered. "Man, take me outta here—please?" I darted a glance at the woman and recognized the lips. Barbeque Woman, not Tiger-skirt. Oh no. Sergei started moving toward us, a gun in his hand.

I rolled down the window. "Get the fuck out of here before you get killed," I hissed. She jerked a quick look behind her, saw Sergei coming, and then ran like hell. I didn't blame her. I switched on my engine, planning to run Sergei's ass down.

Suddenly, a car pulled up to the building. Sergei looked back at it, indecision on his face. A door opened and a woman fell out of the car, her dress torn and dirty. Then the Giant got out, collected money from the driver and the car took off, tires screeching. Giant grabbed the woman by her dreads and pulled her to her feet.

From where I sat, the woman looked like shit. Prince cried out, "Charlize!" All I saw was red and revved the engine. Sergei signaled to the Giant and pointed in my direction. I jammed my foot on the gas pedal and roared Sugar in his direction. Sergei scampered out of the way like a rabbit. Giant pulled a long knife out of a holder on his belt and held it to Charlize's neck. I hit the brakes and stopped inches from Sergei; the rear of the car fishtailed, and Prince's head hit the dashboard. When I jumped out of the car, gun in hand, I aimed it directly at Sergei's black heart.

"You shoot me, your girlfriend dies," Sergei said.

I held the gun rock-steady and didn't move a muscle.

"Yuri—" Sergei shouted.

Yuri took his knife and flicked it against Charlize's neck—blood oozed down the side of her neck. Charlize screamed hysterically, "No, no, no."

Sergei said, "You made a big mistake if you didn't bring me something valuable." He kept his gun aimed at me and moved over to Charlize. "You see your girlfriend's face? Eh? That's cum around her mouth. Pretty, ain't it? Valuable property—I hate to give her up. Yet she isn't as valuable as the diamonds you are holding, is she? Make a choice."

Then he pushed Charlize to the ground, and ordered Yuri to rip her panties off. Yuri set the knife between his teeth and jerked

Charlize's body around like a rag-doll as he ripped and pulled. Panties off, he dangled them in the air. Sergei snatched them and threw them at me. Charlize sobbed helplessly and rolled on the ground.

"Take a whiff. How many men you think she's had? And how many more before we're done with her?"

Charlize crawled toward me, her anguished cries renting the night air. "Amos, help me," she said. "You've got to help me—they'll kill me,"

"All right Sergei, I've got what you want," I said. "It's in the trunk; I need to get the keys."

I moved to the driver's side and reached in for the keys. Prince lay knocked out on the front seat. Damn. Still holding on to my gun, I moved quickly to the trunk of the car, opened it and retrieved the coat. "The jewelry is inside the lining," I said. I thrust the coat at him. "Here, trade, now." I yelled to Charlize. "Get up, Charlize, quick."

Charlize's eyes were glued on the coat. She rose slowly, unsteadily. Sergei pushed her forward and snatched the coat and then ran his hands over the lining. He smiled. I steadied her with one hand and tried to push her in the backseat of the car when Sergei said, "Wait." He took Yuri's knife and exchanged it for his gun and started slashing the coat.

When the first pebbles and stones dropped to the street, I jumped into action and tried to hustle Charlize and get us all out of there. Sergei became enraged. He rushed me while I was trying to deal with Charlize, and with one kick knocked my legs out from under me and I fell. Yuri moved in and held a gun to my head.

Sergei was so mad he was foaming at the mouth and screaming. "Where have you hidden them? Tell me," he shouted and he jerked Charlize out of the car by her hair. She skidded and thumped along the ground. Then he kicked and jumped on top of her, pushing her face into the stones. "Eat them," he directed her. When she didn't, he stood up and kicked her again. "Eat them, bitch," he screamed.

Gun pressed against my temple, I was immobilized, unable to do anything.

Charlize keened and began stuffing pebbles in her mouth. I couldn't watch. "Swallow them. Swallow them," Sergei said, and kicked her again. Snot was flying out of her nose; she gagged trying to swallow them and threw up all over herself, flecks of vomit splattering Sergei's pant leg. Like a maniac, he kicked her again and again.

At that moment, the passenger door of my car opened, Prince got out, swayed, and tumbled in a faint to the ground. This was enough to distract Yuri. I swung my hand backwards and caught him in the throat. He stumbled, his fingers clutching his neck. A crack rent the air, and Yuri's body spun back and fell to the ground. Then another crack and another and then a hail of bullets. Sergei looked surprised, his mouth opened, his knees buckled, and he fell over backgrounds and spun like a bowling pin.

The street was chaos—hookers screamed and ran in every direction. I scrambled for my weapon. Where were the shooters? I motioned to Charlize to get in the car, but she staggered to Prince's side and fell on top of him. Blood pooled in the street next to Yuri and Sergei's bodies. I crawled to where they lay. Yuri stared blankly up at the stars, dead. Sergei lay face down, eating rocks. The gun shook in my hand. The tremor moved to the rest of my body. Death. Up close, an awful sight.

Basil approached with five of his men. They carried no weapons, but it was clear who had taken care of Sergei and friend.

Basil nudged the nearest body with his foot and said, "Street soldiers, replaceable, but it'll send a message. You'll be blamed for this, you know. Your name is on the bullet—as long as the diamonds are still missing."

I jerked my head to look at Basil. His truth punched me in the stomach. Police sirens sounded in the distance. Basil was already moving swiftly away. Over his shoulder he said, "Regrettable about Steadwell. Take your friends and leave. Monya—Monya Lubnick, Sugarland Restaurant in Brighton Beach," Basil said.

Basil's men helped me pile Prince, Charlize, and a torn fur coat into the back of Sugar. Then they booked, running. I started my engine. Tiger-skirt appeared out of nowhere and yelled as I backed up the car, "Don't worry, Sugar, I ain't seen nothing."

I spun the wheel and rolled off into the sunrise Day was breaking, and bit by bit, so was I.

Chapter 32

Charlize didn't want to go to a hospital, so Prince and I patched her up as best as we could. Mostly, she needed to rest. Charlize had swallowed only one stone, as far as she knew. And this, too, will pass, she assured us with a pitiful smile.

But the rest of her story came out. Starting with the fact that Dap Jones was her cousin. As children, he lived with her and her mother and other brothers and sisters for years. Even at a young age, he used to involve her in his schemes, she said.

"He always made it sound so good," she said. He convinced her she could make easy money selling the furs. And she did. She got rid of all eighteen, selling them to the black bourgeoisie around town. They split the money fifty-fifty and she got a coat to boot. Her reason? To raise funds for her man. Funds to support Prince's political aspirations. I shook my head. A smart woman doing something stupid. I knew where she was coming from. But she had paid a heavy price.

We both looked at Prince.

Prince stuttered, "I—I didn't know." I eyed him. Ugly thoughts filtered through my head. Had he made it with Catherine? And then the lyrics from a blues standard popped into my head, "*Woman, your husband is cheating on me*—" and knew I couldn't say anything—a severe case of a pot calling the kettle black.

"I promise I didn't know anything about Steadwell until it was too late."

"And Dap gave you eighteen coats to sell?"

She nodded.

"When?"

"The day before they killed him." Pain seized her and Charlize moaned. I rubbed her shoulder in an attempt to comfort. It didn't work. She moaned even louder.

"Better get some sleep," I said, and looked at Prince. "If she gets worse, you'd better take her to the hospital, no matter what she says." I paused. "You'll take care of her?" He nodded and I left.

I wondered at the conversation they would have after I left.

I downed a bitter cup of coffee at a greasy spoon near Bunky's and waited for the shop to open. My eyes leaden, the coffee didn't do it. I nodded out like any junkie. Ten o'clock I was back out on the street and caught Bunky opening and folding back the accordion iron gates that protected his pawnshop.

"One-suit Amos Brown, how you doing?"

"Bunky, it's been years since I had the one suit. I got at least two now."

"Hocked that one suit every other week."

"Not every other week, Bunky."

"No? You could have fooled me."

"Came to pick up something." I showed Bunky the ticket. He methodically keyed open the three locks on the shop's front door and I followed him inside.

"This ain't yours."

"I know. Doing a favor for a friend. She's in jail and worried about her coat, so I'm picking it up for her."

Bunky looked at the ticket, then shuffled to the back of his shop and returned with the coat in his hand. I got nervous when he flopped the coat around like a pancake on the counter, anxious that the hidden stones might make a noise and arouse Bundy's suspicions. I laid one hand across the fur coat to stop Bunky from flipping it. I pretended to stroke it.

"Good fur. Too bad. This could have sold for a lot," he said.

A casual touch, and I felt nothing. Was I wrong? My confidence unraveled and I began to sweat. Inwardly, I prayed, *let me not be wrong*. Super-cool, I said, "Well, Bunky, you can't win every time. You got a bag I can put this in?" I handed over two hundred dollars.

"You see the size of this bear? What kind of bag you think I got for this heavy motherfucker?"

"I can't go out carrying a fur coat over my arm, Bunky."

"Why not?"

I looked around his shop and spotted a suitcase on a shelf. "How about that?" I said, pointing to it. He pulled the suitcase from the shelf.

"Cost you five dollars," he said.

"Two."

Bunky's eyes glittered and he leaned his elbows on the counter. "I'll roll you for it—how's that?"

See, that's how come Bunky ragged on me about the one-suit; he knew I gambled. Bunky always on the hustle, but to test me at ten o'clock in the morning? I hesitated, and that was enough for Bunky. He produced a set of dice, bones yellowed from age, and placed them on top of the counter.

"These are antiques," he said. "From the Civil War."

I doubted it, but they were old, sure enough. I held them in my hand and rolled them back and forth. Then I took one of the dice between my thumb and forefinger by diagonally opposite corners and lightly held it. It tipped downward. I did the same with the other one while chatting up Bunky. "Okay, Bunky, let's do it. You sure you want to take a chance? Hmmm . . . let's see. How about— if I roll snake eyes three times in a row I get the suitcase for two dollars."

"Aww, Amos, ain't possible. Three times? You're on—it's a bet." Bunky's thin rat-face twitched and his hind parts shook in anticipation like a frisky dog.

Like taking candy from a baby. "Yeah, and if I win, you throw the dice into the bargain." Bunky had to think about that one for a minute, but then he nodded. I knelt down on the floor, blew on the bones, and made the first pass. What do you know? Snake eyes.

Bunky groaned, "Aww, man—how'd you do that?" and beat his knees. I threw again. One die settled, the other wobbled, tipped, and then settled. Ones again.

Bunky said, "Amos, you putting voodoo on those dice?"

The third throw Bunky was undone. In good-humored exasperation, he thumped the suitcase down on the counter. "I should of knowed," he said.

"Yeah, you should have. Hey, man, dust the thing off—I ain't buying the dirt—and put the coat inside."

Bunky did as he was told. I threw two bucks on the counter, still smiling.

"See you around, One-suit Amos. Expect I'll be seeing that fur coat again real soon."

But I was out the door. A pity life can't be like those dice—always weighted on your side. At the nearest trash can, I tossed them. That's all my ass needed, to be caught somewhere with a pair of crooked dice on me. I'd be crucified.

Chapter 33

Our friends which art in heaven. Wilbur died on New Year's Day. Miss Ellie draped black across his door, like they used to do in the old days.

Winnie, Miss Ellie, Oscar, and Josephine, and I stood in the hall-way outside his apartment, talking softly.

"He'd be cooking up black-eyed peas today."

"And calling folks. And wishing them Happy New Year."

"And gossiping about who did what to who."

"And we'd be laughing fit to bust."

"And we'd be laughing," I said.

Josephine looked up at us with solemn eyes.

Chapter 34

All day we waited for the coroner's office to show. They never did. Upset, I roamed the rooms of my apartment like an edgy panther, Wilbur's death the last straw in a chain of events that weighed heavy on my mind. It stank, this death. Josephine didn't really get it yet. She was staying with Winnie temporarily.

I did the ordinary things. I sat in front of the television. I drank beer, ate pretzels. The brownstone was quiet, except for the occasional ring of the office phone. People called to ask about Wilbur. My answering machine took their messages.

In the late afternoon, in the deepening darkness of day, I went to the office to take care of paperwork that I'd been neglecting. I turned on the desk lamp and worked steadily for over an hour, pausing occasionally to take a swig of beer or expel a scintilla of emotion. Night overtook day, and finally I sat back in the dimly lit room and allowed myself to drift—that's what my mind had wanted to do all along.

The day I had seen the black hearse roll down the street, I had had a feeling. Prophetic? I thought so. Shades of my father? I hoped not. His voodoo curses still raining down on me? I sighed and rested my head on the desk. Steadwell dead, now Wilbur. An energy in the room swirled around my body and dulled the pain and made it bearable.

It hurts when people leave you. That much I understood. If they're a part of the street scene, they leave faster, more violently, more ugly than anyone else, and that hurts, but its something you can wrap your mind around, something that makes sense in the scheme of things. I understood that—Steadwell would have, too.

But Wilbur's death I didn't understand. What was the point? Wilbur had been a dancer, for God's sake. Did God have something against dancers? And to die of something nobody could put a name to. Gay men's cancer. The weirdest shit I ever heard in my life.

I couldn't get used to the idea of him being gone. Not yet. He'd been like family. A brother, even. A faggoty brother, but a brother just the same. He'd be pissed if he heard me talk about him like that. Well, but that's the point—he's not going to hear me. I balled my fists.

And Steadwell's not retiring to Costa Rica. And when will the hearse come for me? In the midnight hour, if I don't get rid of those diamonds. I stood and looked out the window at the street—mostly deserted, a gray day, the color of an army blanket.

The diamonds and the other jewels had not been in Patty's coat. I pretty much destroyed the lining looking for them. Deflated, I sat on the floor and stared at my rug. But the Russians believed I had them and would come gunning for me. There must be a way out of this. I blocked out everything and began to think. I went to another world, another place. Shades of my father again. When I finally opened my eyes, an hour had passed. My head hurt and my eyeballs ached. I got up to pour myself a glass of water and take an aspirin.

I felt like calling Catherine. But no, bad idea. What for? To cry on her shoulder? To let her cry on mine? To remind her how unfair life was? That both Steadwell and Wilbur had been cheated out of it? I knew that and so did she. And she wants to bring a baby into this unfair world? And would the curse I carried settle like a snake and wrap itself around our baby's shoulder? And what's the point? What's the fucking point?

I ripped an old calendar off the wall—1980 was dead and done. I closed up shop, returned to my apartment and plucked a book off the shelf. Huh, *A Farewell to Arms*. I skipped past the irony, crawled into bed, and lost myself in the book. Heartbreak for a guy named Henry and a heroine named Catherine. How about that? Just what I needed. Disillusionment everywhere.

In the wee hours, I got up, placed a call to a blonde. I got the answer I'd been looking for.

They picked up the body the next morning. I chilled until early afternoon. The grapevine buzzed. The word slithered across telephone wires, in bars, beauty shops, on corners. Ghosts, someone said. A gray invasion. Basil warned me. Okay, time to take it to them.

I packed up Sugar, gassed up, and headed out of Harlem into southwest Brooklyn, past run-down bungalows and wood-framed houses nestled in the shadow of the el, whose deterioration matched that of Harlem, another community in decline. An eye-opener—I couldn't believe white people lived like this. Some old people with frightened faces walked down the street, looking over their shoulders, but really, it resembled a ghost town. Stunned, I cruised down Brighton Beach Avenue and felt like a foreigner in my own country. Almost all the signs were in Russian. Russian signs branded shops, restaurants, and bars. People stared as I drove by.

I made a left, and then turned right onto Coney Island Avenue, drove to the address Basil had given me, parked, and got out. People with sour faces frowned at me. I wondered, is this how white people feel nowadays when they come to Harlem? And were we insulated in Harlem—or isolated? Seeing this community made me wonder. The distrust was evident in these people's faces. I saw hardly any young people—some middle-aged thug types hung out, cigarettes dangling from their lips. I jumped out of the car, locked it, and strode quickly into the restaurant before the thugs decided to move.

Inside the restaurant, the entire room jumped to their feet. A standing ovation and I hadn't done anything yet.

"Looking for Monya."

A tank sitting beside the door, with tattoos up the yang-yang and fingers the size of sausages, sat back down and dunked bread into his soup head down, and gibbered in Russian with the rest of the room. The others resumed their seats and gibbered back. They didn't look at me, either. Tank paused between bites of bread to put a hurting on a bottle of vodka. I knew I was being ignored.

"That's fine, my friends, but I wouldn't want to be in your shoes when Monya finds out I was here and you didn't tell him. Amos Brown. He should know the name." I turned to go, and Tank held out an arm to stop me.

"Wait here," he said.

I sat and politely asked a waiter for a bourbon and water. No one served me. "Vodka?" I asked. Nothing. That's all right. Like the crooked dice, I had jumped into this with the weight on my side. I wasn't worried. Much.

Five minutes later, the man returned and escorted me into a private dining room off the main room. What do you know? I happened upon a game of poker.

A few minutes lapsed. No one said anything. Seven-card stud. Hi-lo. I watched the action and got the idea real quick the players were taking advantage of their boss's bad playing. Two had ganged up on him in a cooperative effort and were killing him.

He puffed on a vile smelling cigar. "Looking for you, Amos Brown, and you show up here. You nuts or what?" he said, except to my ears it sounded as if he said, *nudz. No, I wasn't nudz*, I thought.

"Yeah, I know. Your men stick out in Harlem like I stick out here. Looking for me? Or a couple of million dollars worth of diamonds and such?" The fool held his cards so everyone could take a look at them. I moved around him and adjusted his cards. He looked surprised. "The object of poker is to keep your opponents guessing— exposing your hand is not good poker. Arrange the cards so you know what you've got."

He snarled, and then made a decision about which cards to throw away. He lifted three of them, ready to ditch them. I groaned. The other people around the table objected strenuously in Russian. Monya fired back, louder and stronger. Subdued, they zipped their lips and took it. He had been looking at a pair. I was going for the straight. I tapped a card. He caught on, raised the eight of diamonds from his hand to throw away. I nodded. Now he was getting it. He asked for one card. Looks darted around the table. The card was dealt down and dirty. Oops. He didn't get his card. Never mind. I whispered in his ear, "Keep a straight face. Make a sizeable bet. Bluff."

Monya put on a gleeful face instead, bet big, and watched the reactions from his fellows. They lost heart and folded. Monya scooped in the pot and said to me, "You wouldn't come here if you had it on you. Where is it?"

"Sergei and Yuri a part of your crew?"

Monya smiled. "They're—independents. But related, you know?"

I nodded. "But they were trying to take the diamonds from you."

"In Russia, every man for himself. It happens. Nothing to get upset about.

"Have you thought about who put them on to the diamonds in the first place?"

Monya pulled on his cigar, the smoke drifting lazily in the air. The cards were dealt. This time Monya kept them close to his chest. He didn't answer, but I could hear the wheels turning in his head.

"Cherchez the coats."

"What?"

"That means . . ."

"I know what it means—Brown. I was a professor in my country."

Step back, I thought. Huh. An educated mobster. Didn't matter. I held the cards on this, not him.

"Well, think this through, Professor. What's your connection to Ralph Evinrude or whatever his name is?"

Monya narrowed his eyes. "Former KGB."

"He set up the deal with you, right? And stitched the stones in the coats. Did you know he also set up the play for the coats to be snatched? But he always intended to get them back and carry out the plan on his own. He double-crossed his boss and he double-crossed you. You feeling me so far?"

Monya leaned forward, about to make a bet. I winced. He looked at me, retracted the bet, and checked. I smiled. The other Russians grew vocal again. "Hey," I said, "you've been cheating him up to this point—it's time he got his back." Anxious eyes darted around the table. Monya had a murderous look in his eye, but he smiled expansively and resumed play. The next two hands he won. The third, he lost and looked to me. "Win some, lose some," I said.

He hesitated and then he smiled and repeated, "Win some, lose some."

Right now I felt I had an edge, so I pressed. "I figure, those diamonds are on their way to Russia by now. What do you think? But I'd be willing to bet he kept a few baubles around his pad—for whatever. Maybe to gift his ladies? Pay a visit to his Manhattan apartment and find out. Are you game?"

I moved to go. "Well, it's been great doing business with you. You want some more poker lessons, call me anytime."

They started yakking that Russian gibberish and I left, hopped into Sugar and headed back home. I opened the car window and let the breeze coming from the ocean refresh me. Funny, it didn't stink so much out here now. I waved to an old man. He teetered off his cane and almost fell over from shock. Hey, I was all about loving my fellow man.

Cruising back home, a black Lincoln passed me, roaring down the expressway. I could have sworn it carried a bunch of Russians. Poor Ralphie.

I made one more stop.

Went to Riverside Park and checked in with Sidewinder. He deserved to know what had happened to his friend. Took it pretty well, but blamed all that happened on the love of money and urged Steadwell's stash on me. He had no use for it, called it the devil's money. I figured, if Bunky could fence it, Patty's rehab expenses might get paid.

Like they say, it ain't the money that's evil. It's what men do to get it—hoard it, keep it, spend it—that's the problem. I slipped the stones in my pocket.

Chapter 35

A flurry of phone calls tied up my line. People checking to see if I was still alive. The last call stumped me. Captain Bundt phoned with instructions to meet him at a place on St. Nicholas in a half-hour. A cop hangout, he said, but informed me that some of *my kind* would be there too. He hung up too quickly for me to question what he meant, but it didn't sound good, this meeting. Unease settled over me like a scratchy blanket. I had a feeling. Some kind of trap?

I dressed carefully—gray-striped pants, button-down dove-gray shirt and tie. I didn't know what kind of place it was. If he wants to see me so bad, let him wait. This boy wasn't going to jump when he called. The phone rang. I let it. Over the answering machine I heard Catherine's voice. I kept on dressing. No sir, not jumping, not me.

I shouldn't have bothered. The place was a dive, but packed to the gills—an old-boy hangout. Split fifty-fifty, full of cops and criminals. All of them joking, telling lies, and acting chummy. Although from the looks of it, they weren't acting—they *were* chummy. Well, when you think about it, both elements had a lot in common, so why not commingle? The question was—how did I rate getting invited to this fraternity of folks?

I spotted Bundt at the bar. He was in his cups and feeling jovial—still, I didn't trust his conviviality. Something was up.

He motioned me to a spot beside him. I adjusted my tie and my jacket and put a foot up to the bar.

Face flushed, Bundt ordered the bartender to give me a drink. Hell, that gesture on his part should have made me run for the door, but I didn't. Curious, I waited for the surprise Bundt was about to spring.

He turned to the guy next to him. "Skip, get out your pad and pencil. You're about to question a suspect, hear?

My heart turned over. I'm about to be arrested, and I got dressed for this? Drunk, Skip did a five-minute vaudeville act on getting out pad and pencil. When he finally got it together, he licked the tip of his pencil and said, "Shoot."

Chicago against Green Bay was on the tube and the noise in the place had reached decibel levels. Every conversation a shout-out.

"Don't I get read any rights?"

"If you want, sure. Go, Skip."

Skip slurred, "Whatever you say is gonna be used against you . . . Is that enough?"

"Sure, that's enough. Hey, Brown, somebody said they saw you in conversation with the Russians at Wells' last week. You know, the ones that got shot—what's their names?"

My insides turned over. Visions of me doing hard time made my stomach dance. The cops had connected me to Sergei and Yuri's shootings? "I don't know what you're talking about," I said.

Bundt smiled and patted me on the arm. "Good answer, good answer." He leaned over to Skip. "Write that down."

"Got it."

The dove-gray shirt stuck to my body. I kept my eyes glued to Bundt. Was this a joke? His eyes rolled around in his head. How long had he been in here?

"Yes, and furthermore, somebody—and we're not saying who—somebody recognized your car at the scene of the crime."

"That's crazy."

"Right, right, and why is that?"

Confused, I repeated, "Why is that? I don't know—"

Bundt put his fingers to his lips, and shushed me and said, "Because . . ." He waved his hand, indicating I should repeat after him. "Because . . ."

"Because . . ."

"You were having a drink with me at Powell's bar."

"I was having a drink with you at Powell's bar?"

He turned to Skip. "Isn't that what I just said?"

Skip wasn't listening. He had fallen asleep, his head on the bar.

"Never mind. That's your story, and you're going to stick to it, right? And who'd take the word of a hooker against an upstanding citizen like yourself? Huh? Brown, we should have had you on the force. You keep going like this, you'll clean up Harlem."

Okay, so it took me a minute, but I finally got it. "Word up, okay, that's the story I'm sticking to."

"Because nobody, no Russian Jew bastards, are going to take over my turf, *my* Harlem," Bundt said. "Not if I have anything to do with it."

Oops. I raised an eyebrow. I'm sure somebody else did, too. The bar got quiet in the vicinity of where we stood. Then, the ebony bartender with frizzy hair said, "Watch your mouth, Captain—my mother is Jewish."

Bundt turned bleary eyes toward him and said, "Yeah? Not talking about you—or your mother. It's the foreigners I'm talking about. What I mean is, Harlem is for niggers, right? Keep the white asses out, right?"

This time quiet rippled through the entire crowd and a hush settled. Disturbed glances flicked back and forth among the men. The cops started closing ranks, and the brothers, in turn, started bunching together. Drunk and unconcerned, Bundt had his arm wrapped tight around my shoulder—hard for me to move. Then all of a sudden a Puerto Rican brother slid two fingers between his teeth, let out a piercing whistle, and yelled, "Harlem for niggers. Keep the white asses out." Spics and Spades, and Micks and 'Ricans and Africans, and Islanders in the room began to take up the chant. Some played the top of the bar like a congo drum. Somebody who didn't get it threw a punch, which provoked a few others to leap into the fray.

This was crazy. Ain't messing up my good vines over this shit. See, this is what happens when cops and criminals get friendly. The Wild West. Time for me get hat. As I exited through the door, crashing glass tinkled behind me.

My Harlem, dammit. Somebody ought to call the police.

Chapter 36

Tranquil, quiet, a stream bubbled nearby. Patty stood on the terrace of the facility, overlooking a forest of trees. We had stepped outside, at my insistence, for Patty to puff on a cigarette. Everybody smoked in the place. The staff, the doctors, the patients. My thinking—if the drugs didn't get them, the nicotine sure would, but I held a minority opinion.

I watched Patty puff. She looked better, her eyes brighter, her face more open.

"So what happened to him?"

"Who?"

"Ralphie."

"He skipped. Got away clean. Figure his wife and father-in-law are still wondering what happened."

"And his girlfriend?"

"Hazel? I got a postcard, stamped Rio de Janeiro. Not with Ralphie anymore. I suspect she ended up with the jewelry." The air up here blew crisp and clean in my face. I inhaled the freshness. "Monya got indicted on a federal rap. Racketeering. I don't think it's going to stick. He called me for poker lessons."

All Patty had on was a cable-knit sweater, and she shivered and puffed some more. "Wilbur never liked Texas," she said.

"No? What made you say that?"

"Texans didn't care much for homosexuals. Growing up, people made it hard for him down there."

"Yeah, well. Some people are ignorant."

Patty slid her eyes at me. "Thought you didn't like 'em, either."

I colored. "I liked Wilbur—he was all right."

"They got some homosexuals in this place."

"Yeah?"

"Sick, too. They getting off drugs, but it ain't doing them no good. They still sick. Some people think it be from the needles." She sighed. "I'm sorry about Wilbur. He was real good with Josephine."

"He was good period." I paused. "You know you have to get well. Josephine needs you."

Tears filled Patty's eyes. "I know. I miss my baby. I think about her all the time."

"She's doing fine with Catherine."

"Ain't the same as having her mama with her."

"No. It ain't."

"But I'll be out soon. A halfway house, then home."

I blew on my hands—should have brought my gloves—left them in the car. I looked at the mountains in the distance. Beautiful up here, and yet I already missed the bustle of the city. There were few black people in this facility, and I missed seeing the colors, shapes, sizes of the people of Harlem. Their voices were calling me.

"Well, I gotta go," I said.

"Think maybe I'll go someplace like Texas, where they got space all around and you can see for miles in every direction. Wilbur used to tell me about it. A place where I can get away from—you know—bad influences."

"Didn't you go to California to do that? And what happened? Patty, you carry yourself with you wherever you go. Can't get away from yourself. And yourself is what's making you take the drugs, not the place."

"It's harder in Harlem."

I couldn't argue with that. "You're right. Only the strong survive. Whatever you decide."

"School, maybe."

"That's possible. Well, look, I got to go."

"Heading back to Harlem?"

I straightened my cap on my head. *Where else?*

DOWN AND DIRTY

GAMMY L. SINGER

ABOUT THIS GUIDE

The suggested questions are intended to enhance your
group's reading of this book.

DISCUSSION QUESTIONS

1. Given what you know about the characters, what do you think happens to Patty? To her daughter?

2. How has opinion changed over the decades since the public first became aware of the AIDS epidemic? Has your own opinion changed about the disease or the victims of the disease?

3. What character do you identify with or have some sympathy for? Why?

4. Is Amos a good "catch"? Why or why not? Would you want your daughter to marry him? Similarly, would you want your son to marry Catherine? Why or why not?

5. What evidence of racism do you see in the context of the story? How does it shape the characters or events?

6. Do you foresee Amos and Catherine getting together?

7. Amos is optimistic about the future of Harlem. Is your opinion negative after reading this book? What details of the story shaped your opinion? Can two people living in the same place have totally opposite experiences? That is, is Amos' Harlem the same as others' living during the same time period?

8. If you were to cast this book as a film, what actors would you put in the lead roles?

9. Can people who do bad things be considered good people and vice versa? What do you think about Basil?

10. What characters seem to be a product of their environment, or does that idea no longer have any validity? Are we entirely in control of our own destinies or do place, time, and other people shape our lives?

11. People continue to survive in dire circumstances, but why would someone like Sidewinder choose to live underground? What are his reasons? Do you believe him?